ADRIFT IN TIME

## OTHER BOOKS BY JOHN WILSON

*Weet,* 1995, Napoleon Publishing

*Weet's Quest,* 1997, Napoleon Publishing

*Weet Alone,* 1999, Napoleon Publishing

*Across Frozen Seas,* 1997, Beach Holme Publishing

*Ghosts of James Bay,* 2001, Beach Holme Publishing

*Lost in Spain,* 2000, Fitzhenry & Whiteside

*North With Franklin: The Lost Journals of James Fitzjames,*
1999, Fitzhenry & Whiteside

*Norman Bethune: A Life of Passionate Conviction,*
1999, XYZ Publishing

*John Franklin: Traveller on Undiscovered Seas,*
2001, XYZ Publishing

*Righting Wrongs: The Story of Norman Bethune,*
2001, Napoleon Publishing

*And in the Morning,* 2003, Kids Can Press

*Flames of the Tiger,* 2003, Kids Can Press

*Discovering the Arctic: The Story of John Rae,*
2003, Napoleon Publishing

*Dancing Elephants and Floating Continents,*
2003, Key Porter Publishing

# Adrift in Time

John Wilson

RONSDALE PRESS

ADRIFT IN TIME
Copyright © 2003 John Wilson

RONSDALE PRESS
3350 West 21st Avenue
Vancouver, B.C., Canada V6S 1G7
www.ronsdalepress.com

Edited by Veronica Hatch
Typesetting: Julie Cochrane, in Minion 12 pt on 16
Cover Art: Ljuba Levstek
Cover Design: Julie Cochrane
Author Photo: Tom Shardlow
Paper: Ancient Forest Friendly Rolland "Enviro" — 100% post-consumer
    waste, totally chlorine-free and acid-free

Ronsdale Press wishes to thank the Canada Council for the Arts, the Government of Canada through the Book Publishing Industry Development Program (BPIDP), and the Province of British Columbia through the British Columbia Arts Council for their support of its publishing program.

**National Library of Canada Cataloguing in Publication Data**
Wilson, John (John Alexander), 1951–
    Adrift in time / John Wilson.

    ISBN 1-55380-007-9

    I. Title.
PS8595.I5834A75 2003      jC813'.54      C2003-910330-7
PZ7W696Ad 2003

At Ronsdale Press we are committed to protecting the environment. To this end we are working with Markets Initiative (www.oldgrowthfree.com) and printers to phase out our use of paper produced from ancient forests. This book is one step towards that goal.

Printed in Canada by AGMV Marquis

*For Fiona Elizabeth Wilson*
*the sister I never knew*
*May 21, 1940–October 23, 1948*

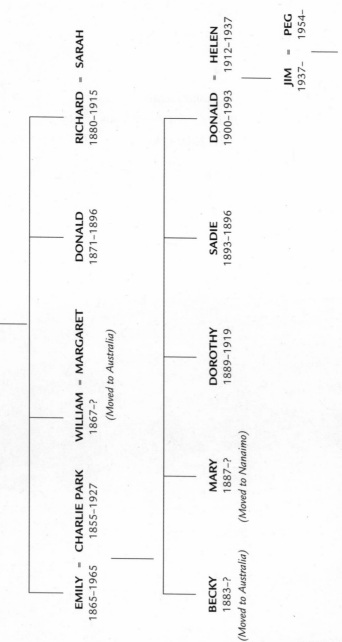

# Ian's Family Tree

IAN MACPHAIL = MARY GUNN
1834–1905        1842–1898

EMILY = CHARLIE PARK
1865–1965   1855–1927

WILLIAM = MARGARET
1867–?
*(Moved to Australia)*

DONALD
1871–1896

RICHARD = SARAH
1880–1915

BECKY
1883–?
*(Moved to Australia)*

MARY
1887–?
*(Moved to Nanaimo)*

DOROTHY
1889–1919

SADIE
1893–1896

DONALD = HELEN
1900–1993   1912–1937

JIM = PEG
1937–  1954–

IAN
1988–

# Chapter One

"I hate this place!" Ian was forcing himself not to shout, but the anger in his voice was obvious. It was also obvious in the way he was pacing about the small room like a caged tiger. His mother sat silently at the rough dining table watching her son. "It might be all right for kids and hippies who don't know the sixties are over, but not for me. I'm nearly fifteen. I've got a life to lead. I don't want to spend every free moment of every summer here."

This wasn't working out as Ian had planned. He knew it was his father who was fanatical about spending holidays at the old family cottage on Mayne Island. He had hoped to enlist his mother's support for letting him return to a real life back on the mainland, but his frustration was getting the better of him. He had to get himself under control. Ian stopped pacing and forced himself to sit down at the table.

"I'm sorry, Mom," he said. "It's just that Dad doesn't seem to understand. He's so into this place and its history that he can't imagine anyone wanting to spend time anywhere else."

"This place is very important to your father." Ian's mother, Peg, was small and wiry. Her hair had been red once, but it was faded now and streaked with grey. She was used to playing the role of mediator in the sometimes tense relationship between her husband and son.

Ian was an only child and he had come along late. Peg had been thirty-four, but Ian's father, Jim, had been fifty-one. At that age it had been difficult adjusting to having a baby around, and now it was equally difficult to adjust to a strong-willed teenager who wanted to go his own way. Peg was adjusting better than Jim.

"I know he goes on sometimes about this place and his ancestors," Peg continued, "but his roots here go deep. This house has been in his family for generations and his grandmother lived here for almost all her life — and she was a hundred-years-old when she died. I think your father feels a little guilty that he left and went to have a career in Vancouver. Perhaps bringing us here at every opportunity is a way of compensating for that."

"Yeah, Mom, but it's not my guilt. I don't want to be tied to this place anymore than he did when he left. There's other things I want to do instead of sitting around here amongst all dad's old ghosts."

"Like what?" Ian's father stood in the doorway. Even on the threshold he dominated the small room. At sixty-six, his hair was grey, but he was still a large man, broad across the shoulders and with a deep chest. One day Ian was going to be like him, but not yet. Ian had the height, already he was close to six feet tall, but there was a lot of filling out to be done before he would take on the imposing presence of his father. Ian groaned inwardly. He had hoped he could finish the conversation with his Mom before his father returned. Suddenly he felt defensive. Why did the presence of his father always seem to put him at a disadvantage?

"Go to the lake for one," he said more aggressively than he intended.

"And hang out with those no-good friends of yours, I suppose," his father interrupted. "Drinking and getting into trouble."

"Dad! Just because a couple of guys in my class were caught drinking and smoking dope at a party, doesn't mean I am going to turn into a crackhead. Those guys are idiots. Everyone knows that. Maybe I made a mistake. It was a dumb idea to go to that party, but I wasn't drinking and, anyway, it was months ago. Aren't you ever going to let me forget it?"

"No. Not until you show me that you are responsible."

"And how the hell am I supposed to do that if you keep me locked up in this broken-down hut on this godforsaken island? If you don't give me a chance, I'll never act responsible." Ian stood up and faced his father. His voice was rising. He didn't want it to but it seemed to have a life of its own. His father affected him that way these days. "I feel like I'm trapped here."

"Don't swear in front of your mother." His father's voice remained calm which infuriated Ian more than ever. "And don't be so melodramatic. There's lots to do on this island. Your ancestors lived here all the year round with none of the fancy gadgets you waste your time on. Your great grandmother Emily lived in this house for nearly a century, most of that time with no electricity or running water. She put up with hardships you cannot even imagine. I was almost thirty when she died and I don't ever remember her complaining. And your grandfather Donald worked all his life, through the Depression and the war to give me, and you, a decent start. I ask you to come for a few weeks in the summer and all you can do is complain."

"Why do you always have to keep throwing my ancestors at me? I'm sick of hearing how saintly great grandma Emily was and how noble grandpa Donald was. They're dead!

"She died more than twenty years before I was born and he was an old man I barely remember. He spat and smelled and scared me. I'm sorry if their lives were hard, but it's not my fault — and it's not my life. The world is different now and this is my time. It's not the world of my ancestors — they've had their time. I am me. I've got my own life to live and I don't want to do it here." Ian was shouting now. He knew he shouldn't, that somehow by doing it he had lost, but he couldn't help himself. It was all so maddening.

Ian's father's face was hard and his fists were clenched into balls by his side. A tense silence grew between the two as they stood staring at each other angrily. Ian's father broke it in a voice that froze Ian's heart.

"Until you can show me," he said, as if his son hadn't spoken a word, "that you can act like a responsible adult, and as long as you keep living under my roof, you will obey my rules and do as I say. Do you understand?"

Ian shook his head in utter frustration. Everything was happening too fast. Ian felt his emotions spinning out of control

"Damn it dad, haven't you listened to a word I've said?"

The cold voice continued, slowly and precisely, "You do not use language like that in this house in front of your mother. You will apologize right now young man."

Ian was pumped up almost unbearably. His hands opened and closed helplessly by his side. He was so angry he was beginning to shake.

"The hell I will!" he screamed as he pushed past his father, through the low door and out into the slanting, evening sunshine. He heard a shouted command to return, but he ignored it as he stormed through the trees. Tears of anger and frustration coursed down his cheeks. Anger at the unfairness of it all and frustration at his lack of control over events and his own emotions.

Ian felt trapped, imprisoned by an old man's obsession with the past. What good was the past? It was the present and the future that Ian was a part of. But he wasn't being allowed to do anything. Why did his parents have to be so old and boring?

Ian burst through the trees, lost his footing, and tumbled down the low bank onto the rocky beach. A large rock dug painfully into his thigh. "Ouch!" he yelled. Pulling himself to his feet, Ian turned to face the blank wall of trees he had just come through. "I'll show you," he shouted, waving a fist impotently in the evening air, "I'll show you."

# Chapter Two

Ian sat with his back against a large cedar trunk and gazed over Active Pass at the sandstone cliffs on Galiano Island. He was calmer now and time had slowed back to normal, but resentment still smouldered deep inside him. To his left the sun was sinking towards the hills on distant Vancouver Island, painting the cliffs a magic golden orange. The sun was warm on Ian's face, but that would change when it set and the thick dark cloud above overwhelmed the sky. Then the evening chill would take over and, if Ian waited that long, he would be glad of the sweatshirt he had draped over his shoulders. It might even rain by the looks of it. A huddle of small boats were still working the narrow western entrance to the Pass, trying to coax a few last reluctant fish from the cold waters.

There was a beauty to this place. Hard as he tried, Ian could not deny it. Now that his anger had waned, he could remember all the happy times he had had here: the endless summer days of swimming and boating and beach combing; the walks across the hills and quiet afternoons reading as the rain drummed on the cabin's roof and windows. He shook his head. But they were little kid memories, and he wasn't a little kid anymore. His body was changing. Pretty soon he was going to have to start shaving and his voice had an annoying habit of racing up and down the scales at the most embarrassing moments. But he could handle all that. He knew what it meant and it was happening to his friends too. What he found difficult was the way his mind was changing inside. His moods would swing from unutterable sadness to overwhelming anger over the smallest trifle, and there was nothing he could do to stop it. That was what made him feel so alone.

His parents were no help. Peg was sympathetic, but she didn't understand. Jim, who should have understood, seemed only interested in disciplining him and telling him how wonderful his ancestors were. What was the point of that? Ian felt adrift in a world he couldn't relate to. Most of his friends seemed to have a lot more in common with their parents than he did. And most of them still had grandparents alive that they seemed to look forward to visiting.

Ian pounded his fist into the dry dirt at his side in frustration. What could he do? He felt as if there was an explosion bottled up inside him just waiting to be released. And what choices did he have? None! Eventually he would have to go back to the cabin and let its claustrophobic walls engulf him again. He shook his head. God, he felt trapped.

Ian was gazing emptily at the opposite shore of the Pass when a flash of red caught his eye. There was someone on the opposite beach. It was a girl. She was wearing a bright print dress and had long, flowing red hair. As Ian watched, the figure bent, picked up something and hurled it out into the water. A black dog, which Ian had not noticed until now, bounded cheerfully into the water in a cloud of spray to retrieve it.

The girl seemed to be so happy. In contrast, Ian could feel his own anger rebuilding. He picked up a stone and hurled it savagely towards the water. The sense of being trapped almost overpowered him. He envied the unknown girl's apparent freedom — to be able to walk on the beach and play with her dog without a care in the world. Ian felt drawn to the scene across the water. Standing, he stepped from the trees onto the sunlight beach. The dog had made it back and was shaking itself vigorously. Laughing, the girl jumped back from the spray and shook her head. The whole scene seemed so carefree. Ian felt an ache within him. Why couldn't his life be that simple?

The girl bent to scratch the dog's ear. When she stood up she looked across the Pass. Instinctively, Ian waved. The girl waved back then turned and ran up the beach towards a large white house nestled amongst the trees.

Ian felt an odd sense of loss. Then self-pity took over.

Why was everyone having such a good time and not him? Why was his father being so mean to him and not allowing him to live his own life? Why couldn't he make his own decisions? He was old enough. Suddenly it became very important to Ian to show his father that he could make his own decisions. The decision itself wasn't important, but making it on his own was. The problem was, what decision could he make on his own in this place?

Ian turned and shuffled disconsolately down the shingle beach. Ahead of him the large arbutus tree where the row-boat was stored leaned precariously out from the bank. It was a beautiful tree, and great for climbing. It was also a wonderful marker when coming back to shore in the row-boat.

Ian stopped in his tracks. That was it — the rowboat. He could take it and row over to Galiano. It couldn't be hard, he had heard stories of how his wonderful ancestors had done it all the time. The far shore looked really close and there was a good hour of daylight left. Plenty of time. There were lots of people he knew on Galiano that would be happy to give him a bed for the night. Once he was there, he would phone home. By then it would be too late to come and get him. He didn't want Peg to be frightened, he only wanted to make the point that he could make decisions on his own. It would also prove that trying to hold him captive on the island wouldn't work. The more he thought about it, the more his idea seemed perfect.

Ian ran up the beach. There was the boat, tucked upside down at the bottom of the bank. It was an old 12-foot, clinker-built affair, not very elegant but stable and practical. Turning it over, Ian retrieved the oars and life jackets. Pulling on one of the jackets, he threw the oars in, gripped the bow and pulled the small boat over the gravel to the water's edge. He felt elated, in charge. He was escaping. Splashing in the shallow water, Ian floated the boat, clambered in, and settled himself on the seat. He secured the oars in the locks and struggled to maneuver the craft into deeper water. He was on his way. The world seemed a beautiful place.

# Chapter Three

Ian was rowing strongly and was almost a third of the way across Active Pass before he noticed that something was wrong. His back was to the beach he was rowing for, but he kept his direction by focusing on the arbutus tree where the boat had been stored. He was getting farther away from it, but the angle was changing, he had to keep turning the boat. Looking over his shoulder, he could see the beach, but it was off to his right. The current must be dragging him through the Pass. He would have to row back against it to reach his goal.

Swinging the boat's bow around until it was pointing almost back along the Pass, Ian began rowing hard. If he could pull himself back past the beach, it would be easy to row into the shore; then the current would be in his favour.

But it wasn't working. Even rowing hard, the shore was still being pulled past him at an alarming speed. Ian felt a moment of panic. What if he were swept out into the Strait? The light was failing and the clouds were gathering for rain. Ian stopped rowing and rested his aching arms and back. He had to think. The beach was out of the question, trying to get there would just exhaust him. He had to use the tidal current to his advantage. Right now it was sucking him to the east, towards the open water of Georgia Strait. The Pass did a 90 degree dogleg before it emptied into the Strait. The coast of Mayne was rocky, but the main harbour and ferry dock on Galiano was around the corner. If he could get close to Mary Ann Point on Galiano, he should be able to pull himself into more protected waters and then into either one of the small bays or all the way round to the ferry dock at Sturdies Bay.

Taking a deep breath, Ian maneuvered the bow of the rowboat back towards the Galiano shore and set to the oars. It was hard work and he could feel the sweat breaking out on his body and wetting his shirt, but he kept at it and occasional glances over his shoulder told him he was making progress. But was it enough? The closer he came to the Galiano shore, the faster the current seemed. The rocks were racing past. The tidal currents in the narrow passes between the Gulf Islands could be deadly; seven or eight knots Ian thought. A rowboat was completely at their mercy when the tide was running. Ian remembered reading how the

Spanish explorer Malaspina's ships had been sucked backwards through Porlier Pass in 1792, much to the terror of the sailors. They hadn't known what to expect. Ian didn't have that excuse. He should have checked the tide situation.

Grunting with effort, Ian pushed those thoughts out of his mind and focused on his task. Blame wouldn't help him now. He concentrated on the rhythm of his job: getting the oars into the water cleanly, pulling with his body not his arms, rotating the oars as he pushed them forward so that they sliced through the air ready for the next stroke. It was mechanical and almost soothing, but it was tiring. Ian's back was aching and his arms felt like lead. But he kept at it, concentrating on nothing but the next oar stroke and the few feet it would take him closer to his goal of sheltered water and a safe shore.

Ian was close to the point now. The darkness was thickening rapidly and lights were going on in the houses along the beach road. He must have been rowing for an hour and he was exhausted and soaked in sweat. Not far now. Was he close enough to the point to be able to pull around it? It looked good. He dared not go much closer for fear of submerged rocks. The lights on shore were moving past very fast. He was off the point now. A little farther and he could begin pulling for the sheltered water. Ian dredged up his last reserves of strength and began pulling harder. The oars were cutting into the water cleanly and deeply, powering the small boat along.

Ian was in the middle of a long, hard pull when his right hand oar wedged between two submerged rocks and was wrenched out of Ian's grasp. Caught completely off balance, he fell hard over backwards into the bottom of the boat, letting the other oar go as he fell. Both oars flew wildly about as the boat spun completely out of control.

Ian was half way back up to a sitting position when the second shock threw him back down. This time, someone seemed to kick the side of the boat. Hard. There was a loud crack of splintering wood. Ian felt a spray of cold water on the side of his face. A chill much colder than that produced by the water ran down his spine. A leak! The boat had sprung a leak. Frantically, Ian rolled over and began searching along the side of the boat for the hole. It was dark, but by following the spray of water with his hand, Ian found the place in the side of the boat. Running his hand along it he found a bulge in the planks. A sharp sliver of wood sliced the edge of his palm and he pulled his hand back in pain. But not before he had felt the leak. A rock had pushed the side of the boat in and water was coming in at a couple of points. Ian cursed his Dad for getting an old-fashioned wooden boat and not an aluminum one. The leak didn't seem too bad — there was not much water gathering in the bottom. The boat was still manageable and he could still make it into the harbour.

Scrambling, Ian grabbed the flailing oars. The oarlocks had prevented them from going over the side, but now he had to get back in control. Hauling himself awkwardly back onto the seat, Ian fought with the boat. The oar that had begun the trouble was broken off halfway up its blade. When he pulled on both oars he slewed to the opposite side. He would have to compensate. At least the spinning of the boat had stopped. Now, to head for the quieter water before the boat swamped. Ian looked up, and almost burst into tears. He had rounded the point. He could see the lights on shore stretching away around several inviting little coves. But they were discouragingly far away and rapidly falling behind. Swinging the boat around, Ian began rowing for all he was worth.

It was totally dark and a steady rain had begun falling before Ian realized he was losing. He couldn't make any headway against the current, even across it. The force was too great and it was sweeping him along towards the open water. His body ached dreadfully, he was unutterably tired, his hand hurt where he had cut it and the handle of the oar felt slick with blood from the cut. To make things worse, several inches of cold water slopped around in the bottom of the boat, making it even more sluggish and freezing his soaked feet. He was trapped: if he didn't bail out the water, the boat would become too heavy to row and would eventually sink or capsize; if he bailed he would have to stop rowing and the current would have him out of the Pass in no time.

Discouraged, Ian stopped rowing and leaned forward to

catch his breath. The boat drifted. When he felt slightly better, Ian shipped the oars and reached into the stern to retrieve the cutaway plastic bottle that served as a bailer. With long, sweeping motions, be began scooping the water from the bottom of the boat and throwing it over the side. The change in motion was a relief and it was not long before the bailer was coming up almost empty. Ian dropped it and looked up. He had drifted into the middle of the channel and was now almost directly in line with the lights that marked the entrance to the Pass. There was no hope of rowing back now. What options did he have left?

The outgoing tide would carry him into Georgia Strait. How far? He didn't know. At least the current would be manageable in the Strait, maybe only about half a knot. It would pull him south, along the shore of Mayne Island. If that happened, and he wasn't too far out, he could probably pull in to a beach somewhere along there. It would be difficult in the darkness, but if he could spot some house lights on a bay, he might have a chance. Almost any wind would spoil his plan though. It would have more effect than the current and could blow his little boat wherever it wanted. But he would have to wait and see. Right now he was still sheltered by the land on either side.

Ian shivered. He was wet through with sweat, sea water, and rain. Reaching behind him, he felt for his sweatshirt where it had fallen from his shoulders. There it was. He groaned out loud as he retrieved the soaking rag. This wouldn't do much to keep him warm. He wrung out as much water as possible and draped it over his head and shoulders. At least it might keep some of the rain off and stop some heat loss. It was going to be a miserable night at best and, in all probability, a dangerous one.

Ian sighed. How could he have been so stupid? He should have known about the tidal currents before setting out, but he hadn't thought. The prospect of escape had blinded him. Being decisive didn't seem so attractive now. He would be grounded for the rest of his life for a dumb stunt like this. But, despite his miscalculation, Ian still felt a grim satisfaction in the way he had handled the crisis so far. He was thinking. He had managed to keep his head and try to think of different solutions as the situation changed. Not that it would do him much good if he drowned. Shrugging, Ian picked up the bailer and removed the few inches of water that had accumulated while he rested. His stomach rumbled in protest at missing supper. This was not going to be a fun night.

# Chapter Four

Out in the Strait, the water was choppy and Ian had to
work to keep the bow of the boat pointed into the
waves. Even so, whenever he put down the oars to bale the
accumulating water out, the boat slewed round and began
tossing uncomfortably. He could feel the wind driving the
rain from the southeast, fifteen knots he estimated roughly,
perhaps gusting to twenty. He watched the lights on shore
carefully, attempting to judge which way he was going. Not
south, that was sure. So the bays on Mayne were no longer
possible. What was the Galiano shore like? There were
beaches, that was good, but few people lived on that side of
the island and it would be a long walk back to civilization if
he landed there. The worrying thing was that the wind
seemed to be pushing him out into the Strait. He would

have to work hard not to be pushed impossibly far from land. Bending over the oars, he struggled to bring the boat closer to the dark shore of the island but the wind, the need to bail, the damaged oar and his injured hand, made it a frustrating task. Mostly he had to be content with just holding his own.

In periods when the rain eased, he could see the glow of Vancouver in the sky across the Strait and the bright spots of the late-season cruise ships heading up to the glacier-filled bays of Alaska. The lights looked warm and inviting, but they were far away and the rain and darkness soon closed back in and held him in his own small, cold, increasingly frightening world.

Hours passed slowly in the darkness. The work kept the cold from eating too deeply into Ian's bones, but still, he couldn't keep from shivering. He had to find a balance between working hard enough to prevent himself being blown far out into the Strait and retaining enough strength to make it to shore. Then he had to be strong enough to walk to find help. The cozy warmth of the tiny cabin certainly didn't seem like something to run away from now. The interior was vivid in his mind: the cobwebbed corners, the uneven floor, the age-darkened wood of the walls, the small windows, the rough stone of the fireplace. The fireplace. If only he were sitting by that fireplace now, wrapped in a blanket and nursing a hot chocolate, he would be the happiest person in the world.

Was this how the early settlers had felt about their basic shelters when they were out in all weathers hunting, fishing, or herding? Perhaps the harder your life was, the less you needed in the way of comforts. The cabin had been built by Ian's great great grandfather in 1863 after he had come back from the gold fields of the Cariboo. His great grandmother, Emily, had been born there, raised a family of five kids in the tiny space, and died there at the age of a hundred. Ian's grandfather, Donald had been born and lived there as had his father before he went off to university, married and settled in Vancouver. Since Donald had died, it had been used for family holidays.

The farm had long ago been subdivided and the cabin had been altered and modernized over the years, but it was still possible to get a sense of life in the original two rooms and kitchen when it was the centre of a working farm and filled with noisy kids. Despite, or perhaps because of, the dulled state of Ian's mind, he could quite vividly imagine what life must have been like back then: noisy, dirty, hard. He was thankful for all the modern conveniences that made his life bearable. If only he could get back to them.

# Chapter Five

A loud noise interrupted Ian's thoughts — a clacking sound. It took him a moment to realize it was his own teeth chattering. He clenched his jaw. It didn't help. Muscles all over his body were jerking involuntarily. Rowing helped a bit, but he felt unutterably weak. His pulse was racing all of a sudden and his breathing was fast. Ian knew what it meant. His father had warned him about just such a situation as this. His core body temperature was dropping. He was in the early stages of hypothermia. In August? Yes, he thought glumly between shivers. Ian remembered reading somewhere that hypothermia was actually more common in summer than winter. It took you by surprise then. And he was a prime candidate. He must have been in the boat for four or five hours by now. Most of that time he had been working hard. He was exhausted, wet through, chilled by the wind, and dehydrated after losing all that sweat.

What happened next? Ian couldn't remember. His sluggish brain was not working efficiently any more. That was another symptom. Gradually Ian realized that he couldn't feel his feet. Looking down he saw ankle deep water sloshing about as the boat was tossed around by the waves. That wasn't good. Why not? Oh yes, the boat had a leak, and even a few inches of water could make it unstable if a wave caught it sideways. He didn't want to capsize. Leaning forward, he reached for the plastic bailer. His hands felt awkward. He fumbled the bailer a couple of times before getting a secure grip on it. It was frightening how quickly the symptoms had come on. Very carefully and slowly, Ian grasped the bailer and began tipping water back over the side. If this was what life was like in the old days, Ian wasn't interested. It was much too difficult and dangerous.

"It wasn't so bad."

Ian froze, puzzled, with the empty bailer held over the edge of the boat. A voice? Out here? It had been thin and reedy, but it had definitely been a voice. Ian looked around him. Hardly surprisingly, there was no one to be seen.

"What?" he asked into the darkness.

"I said that life in the old days wasn't that bad."

Ian dropped the bailer at his feet and spun around. The boat slewed across the front of a wave and water sloshed over the side. No one. How could there be? He was going crazy. He had read about sailors in open boats becoming delirious, but usually that had been in the south seas and after weeks adrift. Hypothermia didn't make you mad, at least not this quickly. Did it?

Taking one last look around, Ian retrieved the bailer and continued his work. That must take precedence so he worked hard, concentrating so that he didn't have to think about what hearing voices meant. When he was finished, he sat up. That was when he saw the old woman. She was small and looked frail, but she sat upright in the stern of the boat not five feet in front of him. She was wearing a long, dark skirt, white blouse and a blue cardigan, which, oddly, didn't appear wet despite the steady rain. Her face was unbelievably old, but the wrinkled skin fitted naturally around the wide smiling mouth. Her hands were folded on her lap and she appeared to be having no difficulty maintaining her balance against the rolling of the boat.

"Hello," she said in the same soft voice Ian had heard before.

Ian's mind was racing, but he could think of nothing to say. His jaw hung open ridiculously.

"Close your mouth," said the old woman, "it's rude and you might drown in this rain."

Automatically, Ian obeyed.

"Who are you?" he managed at last in a cracked whisper.

"Emily Victoria Park," came the soft reply.

Ian knew that name.

"That was . . . You must be . . . Great Grandmother."

"Yes."

"But," Ian continued, fighting to get his mind working properly and make sense of the strange things that were happening to him. There must be a logical explanation. But there didn't seem to be. "You've been dead for," Ian laboured over the calculation in his head, "nearly forty years."

Once more the soft voice. "Yes, I suppose I have."

"It's odd," the ghost of great grandmother Emily continued, "but I don't feel dead. I don't feel anything really."

Ian's jaw had dropped open again. He stared at the figure in the stern. If he looked really hard, he had the impression that he could actually see through her and make out the outline of the boat behind. Certainly she added no weight. A real person would have pushed the stern down and he would have noticed that. She must really be a ghost. Ian shook his head and blinked hard. He must be dreaming or hallucinating or . . . another thought crossed his mind.

"Am I . . . am I dead?" he asked quietly. The ghost laughed, a light tinkling sound.

"You look very alive to me," she said. "A little cold and wet, but very much alive."

"Well," Ian continued, "why are you here?" A slightly puzzled look flitted across the old woman's face.

"I don't really know," she said. "The last thing I remember is lying in bed in my cottage on the island. I had this horrible cold that had got stuck in my chest. Peg and Jim and Donald were there. Oh, the look on Peg's face. She looked so worried and sad. As if it was unnatural for someone a hundred years old to be dying." The ghost paused thoughtfully. "But that's all I remember until I found myself here. But I know who you are," she looked up. "You're Jim's boy. I knew he would have a son, just took him an awful long time to make up his mind about anything. What year is it?"

"Two-thousand-and-three," Ian replied.

"Two-thousand-and-three," Emily repeated the words, savouring each one in turn. "My goodness. A whole millennium. My how time flies. So what are you doing out here on a boat all by yourself. Doesn't seem to be a very smart thing to be doing."

"It was an accident," answered Ian through his chattering teeth. "I was rowing over to Galiano and the tide pulled me out into the Strait."

"That was no accident," Emily interrupted. "That was stupidity. Going into Plumper Pass in a rowboat without knowing the tide — stupidity. Mind, exactly the same thing happened to my brother Billy. He went out fishing by himself and got pulled out and down the coast. Washed up in Bennett Bay and had to walk all the way home next day. Never seen anyone look quite so sorry for himself as he did when he came through that door around lunch time, soaking wet and shivering so hard he could barely stand. And father didn't make him feel any better. He got a good hid-ing that time and afterwards none of us kids were allowed out in the boat without an adult, or at least an older boy, with us."

The ghost seemed to drift off into a reverie of its own. Ian's mind was a confused mess of thoughts and fears. This was impossible. There were no such things as ghosts. Were there? Yet here was his great grandmother, dead for thirty-eight years, sitting in his leaky rowboat, in the middle of the night, in a rainstorm in Georgia Strait. And the ghost didn't seem to have any clearer idea of what was going on than he did. Ian cleared his throat.

"Great grandmother," he began tentatively. The sound of his voice seemed to rouse the old lady.

"What?" she began. "Oh, I'm sorry. I must have drifted off for a moment. And don't call me great grandmother. It makes me sound even older than I am. My name's Emily. You can call me that. What's your name anyway? I can't go on calling you 'boy' all night."

"Ian," said Ian. Emily's smile broadened.

"Ian," she said as if testing the sound of the name. "That was my father's name — your great great grandfather — Ian MacPhail. He was the one that first came to Canada, back when the old century was barely half way through. He ran away from home when he was fourteen years old. He had a brother or sister for every year of his age around the dinner table. That was up in the Shetland Islands off the northern tip of Scotland. A bleak place. Always the wind blowing in off the Atlantic ocean, so strong that it wouldn't even let a tree catch hold. I can remember when father was an old man, how he used to stand and shake his head in wonder at the big cedars and firs on Mayne. They were still a wonder to him all those years later." Emily paused.

"Why did he come to Canada?" Ian felt himself being drawn into the story. What was he like this long-dead man after whom he was named ?

"It was the potato famine. The family was starving."

"But," Ian asked hesitantly, "wasn't the potato famine in Ireland?"

"Yes. That was where it was worst for sure. Those poor people had no other crop to rely on so a million of them died and another million fled to the new world on the coffin ships. But the blight spread all over Europe. In most places there was something else to eat, but where the people were poor, they suffered. In the highlands and islands of Scotland there were oats and a few other crops, but the people suffered nevertheless. Even in the good times there was barely enough food to keep a big family like Ian's fed. If anything went wrong, they were facing starvation."

"But couldn't the government help? Bring in food or something?"

Emily laughed.

"The government? The government didn't care what happened to a poor farmer in Shetland or County Cork. In those days, if you were poor it was your fault and you had better look after yourself and your family somehow or you would end up in the poorhouse and that was no joke. Life was hard."

The modern-day Ian groaned.

"That's what my Dad says all the time. He thinks kids today have it too easy."

"Oh, they probably do. Kids always have it too easy. That's what parents are for. As for being hard. Yes, life was hard, but don't equate hard with bad. We did what we had to do to get by, but we had good times too. My father always spoke fondly of his childhood in Scotland even though it was hard and there was never enough to eat. He was a very big man, like you will be one day, but he had the soft voice of a highlander. He used to sing us children lullabies in Gaelic. He told me once that he never intended to come to . . . "

Emily's voice faded away until Ian couldn't make out the words. He found himself leaning forward to hear better. As the voice faded, the form faded too and the wooden stern of the boat became clearer. Emily was leaving. Feeling both relieved that he no longer had to deal with a ghost and sad that the old lady was going, Ian closed his eyes and slumped exhaustedly forward.

# Chapter Six

A large wave rocked the boat dangerously and Ian jerked his head up. In front of his unbelieving eyes was a floating palace of lights. For a moment, Ian gazed in stunned wonder. Then he realized what he was looking at — the car ferry from Vancouver to Victoria. Ian's heart leapt. He was saved. They would see him, or at least pick him up on radar.

The ferry was heading for the entrance to the Pass. It would miss him by a good 150 metres, but that was close. He could see details of the lights at the windows and the people on board. They must see him. Any minute now the engines would stop and a boat would be lowered to pick him up. But nothing happened, the huge vessel continued its stately course completely oblivious to the boy in the small boat beside it.

Ian screamed and waved his sweatshirt, almost capsizing the boat with his efforts to stand and make his profile larger. Nothing worked. Of course not. He was dark, low in the water in a choppy sea, and he had no light. They would have seen him on radar but probably thought he was just one of many, mostly sunken, logs adrift in the Strait, and since there was no danger of the ferry colliding, had not checked it out. The ferry must pass dozens of logs on each voyage. The ferry's horn sounded as it approached Active Pass. Ian slumped in his seat. He felt like weeping. That had been his best chance. He still might be spotted by a fishing boat or someone cruising at night, but it was unlikely. The weather was too miserable for many people to be out by choice, and the ferry had shown dramatically how difficult it was to spot a small boat low in the water. Ian collapsed back into lonely misery.

"Laddie," a strangely accented voice said. "You'll want tae watch oot fer yon wake."

"What?" Ian jerked upright and stared at the large figure of a man sitting, apparently comfortably, where Emily had been a few moments before. He was broad shouldered and powerful but, like Emily before him, he lowered the stern not an inch. He was dressed in a suit of coarse woolen material. The jacket was open but a high-necked waistcoat of the same rough material was firmly buttoned up. The white shirt was also buttoned, at least to beneath the thick white beard that hung from the face. The face itself was rugged and stern and the eyes deep set. A mop of white hair complemented the beard and flowed out over the large ears. An incongruous touch of formality was provided by the gold watch chain stretched across the waistcoat and the white handkerchief, neatly folded, in the jacket pocket. A pair of the largest, roughest hands Ian had ever seen lay casually on the figure's lap.

"I said, you'll want tae watch oot fer the wake from yon big ship."

Gradually what the old man was saying dawned on Ian. He glanced to the side. A huge wall of water was racing towards him. Oh no! The wash from the ferry. It was big enough to swamp his small boat if it caught him sideways. Frantically, Ian worked the oars, swinging the bow around to face the onrushing water. Just in time. The bow dipped then shot up the large wave, over the top, then plunged down the other side. Three times the boat did this while Ian worked feverishly to keep it stable. Through it all the figure of the old man sat impassively watching Ian's work.

At last the water quieted and Ian breathed a sigh of relief. Being in the boat was bad enough, being in the water would be deadly.

"Who are you?" Ian asked, turning his attention to his strange visitor.

"Ian MacPhail," the man replied, "and are you no taught manners these days? When I was your age I was taught tae thank someone who helped you."

"Oh! Thank you," Ian stuttered. "The boat would have swamped if you hadn't warned me."

"Aye, it would that," the old man agreed.

"You must be Emily's father," Ian said.

"Aye."

"The one who left Scotland to come here because of the potato famine."

"Aye lad," Ian MacPhail replied, "but I didnae intend tae come tae this wild land. I just went on the whalin' ships for a couple o' years to make some money. You want a hard life? That was a hard life. Workin' through the ice packs in Davis Strait and Baffin's Bay, the ship glistenin' like a weddin' cake in the midnight sun frae a' the ice hangin' on her rails and riggin'. Us men workin' like slaves tae pull her through the ice when the wind wasnae right, fightin' tae cut the ice doon afore she overturned wi' the weight. An' then there were the whales. Great beasts they were that could smash a long boat like match sticks if they'd a mind to.

"Once, we found a cove where the whales came and no one else knew aboot it. That time we could run the creatures intae the shallow water, haul them ashore and render them doon tae blubber oil tae fill oor barrels and head for home. We had tae be rapid, mind. If you were too slow, the ice had you. Maybe you could cut a way oot, maybe you could walk tae another ship, maybe you couldnae. Then you were done. Maybe someone would find your boat the next season, but that was too late tae be any help tae you.

"The second season I was up there, they were lookin' for yon man Franklin an' his crews. Lost they were, up in the Northwest Passage somewhere. We were told tae look oot for any signals frae the shore and tae inquire of any of the Esquimaux we came upon if they had seen any white men in ships. We never found oot anythin', but then neither did anybody else. They just disappeared. All they ever found were bones and some Esquimaux stories aboot the poor sailors eatin' wan another."

"It was lead poisoning."

"What?"

"It was lead poisoning," Ian repeated, "from the tin cans that the food was in. That's what we now think killed Franklin and his men."

"So, did they no' eat each other?" the older Ian asked.

"Oh, yes they did. Researchers have found knife marks on some of the bones. But they were already poisoned by the lead."

"Well," the old man went on in an annoyed voice, "they didnae eat each other because o' the canned food. They ate each other because they were starving — and because o' the North drivin' them mad. That's whit I wis sayin'. That's what the north will do tae you, strip off all your civilization and swallow you up wi'oot a trace.

"It was enough for me. As soon as I got back tae Scotland, I joined a ship goin' aroon' the Horn tae the Pacific. They said there was gold tae be found in California, an' I thought that would be a better life than haulin' carcasses o'er the ice floes. So I went. Jumped ship in San Francisco and headed inland, that would hae been in '49. Of course, most of the easy gold was gone by the time I got there, but there were still a lot o' men like mysel', hopin' there was a good life lyin' aroon' on the ground."

The old man stopped talking and his gaze lowered to Ian's feet.

"An' you, young man," he continued at last, "had better start wi' yon bucket or, come the next wave, we'll both be at the bottom o' the ocean."

Ian doubted that, should the boat sink, the ghost of his ancestor would actually be going down with him, but he saw his point. His mind was reeling with questions about death and heaven and hell and time travel and he had to concentrate hard to understand the old man's heavy accent, but he set to with the bailer, working at the four or five inches of water which had accumulated. As he worked, the old man kept up his monologue.

"As soon as I got tae the gold fields, I knew I wasnae goin' tae find an Eldorado, there was too many hopers there already and all the best creeks were claimed. But there was money tae be made if you'd a mind. A' the miners and prospectors needed places tae sleep and food tae eat, so I opened a stoppin' hoose on the way tae the goldfields. It was sma' at first, just a shack wi' a couple o' rooms oot back and a table in the parlour where I could serve meals. But it was better than sleepin' on the trail, so I sometimes had three or four men sleepin' in each room. I built more rooms and even had a proper dining room put in.

"I did that for a good ten years. Then word came that someone had found gold up in a place called the Cariboo. The gold was long gone from California by then and the place was becomin' too busy for ma likin', so I thought I would try ma luck up there. I did the same thing — started a stoppin' hoose on the trail."

Ian was enthralled now, imagining the exciting lives these people had had. Going off and searching for gold and adventure. They were free. No one forced them to go somewhere they didn't want. If they didn't like something, they just moved somewhere else. That was what Ian had tried to do. It hadn't worked very well, but he had tried. If only there were still gold rushes to run away to.

"That's how I came tae meet your great great grandmother Mary," the old man went on. "She came tae work in the kitchen. I'll never forget the first time I saw her, standin' over the range cookin' bannocks. She wasnae tall, nae mair'n five feet, but she was wiry and quick. The first thing I noticed was her long black hair fallin' a' over the place. I called out tae tell her tae tie it up, I didnae want the customers complainin' aboot the hair that wasnae theirs floatin' in the soup, and she turned aroon'. She was a Lillooet and she had the high cheek bones and chiseled features o' a' her people. She wasnae beautiful mind, at least no by the standards I had been brought up wi', but there was somethin' aboot her eyes. They were black as coal and as deep as the ocean. I fell intae those eyes right then and in forty years

I never found ma way oot again. Not that I tried too hard mind. I was twenty-six when we first met and she wasnae mair than sixteen. We were both lonely, away from home, and tryin' to make oor way in the world. It was natural we should get together, but even when we were both old and had grandwains o' oor ain, she just had tae turn those black eyes o' hers on me and I was a damn fool boy again.

"We made a good go o' the stoppin' hoose and, wi' my savin's frae California, could put a wee bit money aside. Eventually, the hopers stopped comin' and the business slowed doon just like it had done afore. Some o' the miners used tae tell me aboot an island they went tae spend the winter. It sounded good. We had enough saved for a pre-emption on a small farm if we didnae go too close tae Victoria, and I missed the ocean sorely. The miners told me it was possible tae live for nothin' off the deer, birds and shellfish. 'When the tide goes oot, the table is set,' one o' them told me. So Mary and me moved doon and pre-empted a hundred acres on Mayne Island. We . . . "

"A hundred acres!" the young Ian couldn't hide his amazement.

"What?" the old man looked sternly at his distant relative. "Aye, you'll be thinkin' a hundred acres is a fair wee bit o' land. Well so it is, but it wasnae a farm when we took it in 1862. It was raw land, covered in the largest trees you could imagine. We had the devil's own job clearin' even a few acres tae plant some vegetables, never mind startin' a farm. The first few trees we split for the wee cabin, but most o' the wood we burned."

"You burned all the wood?" Ian was horrified at the waste.

"Aye," his great great grandfather peered challengingly over at the boy from beneath a pair of bushy white eyebrows.

"But wasn't that an awful waste?" As time progressed, Ian was feeling steadily more comfortable in the company of ghosts and the story was undeniably interesting.

"A waste?" old Ian laughed. "What else was there tae do? No one logged on any of the islands for many years and we had tae make some fields or else we'd no hae a farm and we might as well hae gone back tae the Cariboo. We cut doon the big trees, bored holes in the trunk every six or eight feet, filled the holes wi' pitch and set it alight. We could burn the biggest tree in twa days that way. That was the easy bit; the work was in the stumpin'. We used oxen for the heavy haulin' work and for pullin' the stumps oot. Gradually we cleared the land and got tae plantin'. The wains come along pretty quickly too. Emily was the first in '65. Mind, we'd almost left after the murders the year afore."

"Murders?"

"Aye, poor old Marks and his daughter. The family was crossin' Plumper Pass . . . "

"Plumper Pass? Emily mentioned that. Was that Active Pass?"

"Aye. They didnae change the name for the longest time. The old timers still used Plumper through the Great War. Noo, if you keep interruptin', you're no goin' tae hear the story."

"Sorry," Ian was contrite.

"Aye well, the Marks family were comin' over frae the San Juan Islands in twa boats, Mrs. Marks, the four wee ones and the skipper in one boat and Mr. Marks and his married daughter in the other. Caroline her name was. She couldnae hae been more than fifteen, just a lass."

"Married! At fifteen?" Ian couldn't stop the question coming out. His ancestor looked at him sternly.

"Aye, fifteen and married. What was the point o' waitin'. Young folk knew what they wanted in those days — and they knew when tae hold their tongues when their elders were talkin'.

"Noo, as I was sayin'. There was a storm and the boats was separated. The skipper managed tae get his boat in tae Miner's Bay on Mayne, but Marks and his daughter were washed up near Croker Point on Saturna. It seems they were set upon by a band of Lamalchi Indians and murdered. They never found the bodies only the boat, a campfire and their twa dogs. The navy brought in a ship, H.M.S. *Forward,* I think, and she bombarded a few villages. Did a lot o' damage but the only person killed was a sailor by a shot frae the shore. They arrested a band o' people, and hanged four men ootside the police barracks in Victoria. That settled things doon a bit, but there was a lot o' fear aroon' that time. The settlers were just a handful and some o' the Indians were a warlike lot, takin' off the heads o' their enemies and such like. If they had a mind to, they could hae killed every single one o' us inside a week and there would hae been nothin' anyone could dae aboot it."

"But the settlers were stealing the land that belonged to the First Nations."

"Hah!" the old man's derisive laugh echoed through the darkness. "Stealin' is it? Aye, maybe later on when there was a lot o' folk settlin' and the Indians were put on the reserves, but when Mary and me went tae Mayne, there wasnae any stealin'. The land was empty. The Indians lived on the coast and travelled all over in their canoes from bay tae bay huntin' and fishin'. There was plenty room for everyone in those days. What mostly frightened us was the way the Indians treated each other. I met a Hudson's Bay man once who told me how he had come upon a massacre up the big island at Qualicum. A whole village was wiped oot and the bodies horribly cut up, the heads was a' taken off and put on spikes. Women and bairns too. None o' us wanted oor heads tae end up that way. The only protection we had was the navy.

"The *Ganges* came up this way before I moved doon. She was a big ship, eighty-four guns. She must hae put the fear o' God intae anyone who wanted tae cause trouble, even those uppity Americans wi' their 'Fifty-four Forty or fight' nonsense. But, even the two guns o' the like o' the *Forward* were enough tae deter the Indians from becoming too troublesome. Of course, there were some people who would like tae hae seen the Indians moved away and cleared oot, but most o' us was happy enough tae live and let live as long as oor heads wernae in danger."

"Your wife must have been very scared," Ian interrupted with the image of dozens of Indians' heads on spikes still vivid in his mind.

"My wife?" Old Ian seemed puzzled for a minute. "Oh Mary! Mary wasnae my wife. At least no until I went tae work on the lighthoose and that wasnae afore '80 or '81. I had tae get the papers then tae work for the government. No, most o' us old-timers never paid much mind tae the paper marriages.

"Anyway, it was a hard life, but we got by. I mind I used tae go huntin' for deer meat to sell in Victoria and New Westminster. That brought in a few dollars to help wi' the farmin'. And then there was the work on repairin' the old steam engines. I always seemed tae have a knack wi' that sort o' machinery. There was one time . . . "

"That's enough, Ian. Bending the poor boy's ear with your fearful stories of heads put on spikes. He wants an idea of what life was like — not death." The soft sounds of Emily's voice wafted over from somewhere undefined.

"But death was a part o' it too. You couldnae appreciate life wi'oot realisin' that the other was sometimes close at hand. Now I've got a lot more stories that the boy should hear if he's ever goin' tae . . . " The lilting highland voice faded away as the figure appeared to melt before Ian's eyes. If you had asked him afterwards, he would not have been able to say exactly when the change occurred, but all at once, Emily was back, smiling at him with her friendly, wrinkled face.

"He's a lovely man," she said, "but he can go on terribly once you get him started."

# Chapter Seven

"Emily," Ian asked, "why is this all this happening?"

"I'm not sure," Emily looked a bit puzzled. "I just found myself in the boat with you. I thought I should start talking so you wouldn't be too scared, and all I can remember is my life on Mayne, so that is what I talked about. I don't know if there is any purpose to it."

"There must be," Ian sounded quite forceful. "Either I'm going crazy, or I'm dying, or you and old Ian are here for a reason. Maybe you're here to tell me about the past. I've mostly ignored it, but perhaps it is important. I don't know."

"Oh, it is important — very. And the past becomes more important the older you become. When I was sick in the cabin, everyone was so worried that I was suffering, but I wasn't. I was reliving my life, my childhood years. Mayne was really the best place in the world to be a child in those days and I loved it. We children ran free all the time. There wasn't even a school to go to until Mrs. Monk began one in 1883. It was too late for me, I was eighteen and married by then and had a baby of my own."

"Eighteen?" Ian couldn't hide his surprise. "Did everyone marry that young?"

"Yes," Emily's smile broadened. "Most did. You had to get going on your life in those days. Get married and have children so they could help you run the farm. You weren't a child for very long before you had to begin helping with the chores and earning your keep, but for the few years you were a child it was a wonderful life."

"It was that, Emily. Do you remember me teaching you to shoot deer with the old rifle?"

A second figure had appeared beside Emily. It was a young man, in his twenties, Ian guessed. He had a broad smile beneath a mop of dark unruly hair.

"I do Billy, and I think I still have the bruises on my shoulder from the recoil." Emily answered.

The new arrival laughed. "But the teaching was good, Emily, you became a good shot, and we made a pretty penny or two selling the deer meat you brought down."

"And more from the fat grouse we used to sell to the steamer passengers out in the Pass," Emily added.

"And the starfish," continued the newcomer, "sold for fertilizer at 50¢ a hundred."

"Yes, I remember," said Emily happily, "but we're being rude. We need an introduction. Ian, this is my brother William."

The young man's ghost bowed formally. "Pleased to meet you. I see you are in something of a similar predicament to the one I once got into. Do you remember, Emily?"

"I do, Billy, and I have already mentioned it to Ian as a cautionary tale on not taking the waters of the Pass seriously enough."

"Bah," Billy dismissed Emily's warning, "the Pass is all right, the Strait too. You just have to keep your head and all will be fine. People rowed the Pass all the time. Some even swam it — do you remember the time I was taking the old cow round to the back pasture in the boat and she got spooked. Jumped right out of the boat and swam clear across the Pass. I had the devil's own job finding her and loading her back into the boat. We had some good times, did we not?"

"Yes," agreed Emily, "but it was not all jolly and carefree. What about poor Mrs. Swan?"

"Yes, that was very unfortunate. But these things happen. We cannot always avoid them."

"Who was Mrs. Swan?" Ian had been watching the to-and-fro between the ghosts with interest.

"Mrs. Swan was the mother of Annie, my best friend," said Emily turning to face Ian. "They used to row over from Galiano and stay the night. I loved those occasions because

I got to play with Annie instead of my brothers," she glanced back at Billy who reacted with a broad wink. "We all got to stay up late and then had to cram into the one bed as best we could. There was me, Billy, Donald, who was just a baby, and Annie who was one year older than me."

The name Donald struck a note with Ian. Great grandma Emily had a brother Donald, his great uncle. Before he had a chance to ask anything, Billy interrupted.

"We always used to draw straws," he said, "to see who would sleep beside Donald, because he used to wet the bed sometimes and the person beside him always got soaked."

"And it was always me who seemed to get the straw on the nights he had an accident," Emily was smiling broadly but it faded as she sat in silence for a minute.

"The last time Mrs. Swan and Annie came over," she continued eventually, "began just the same as all the others. It was only the next day when they rowed back that they discovered the tragedy. Poor Mr. Swan had been killed. Shot in the back as he was splitting logs in the yard, and while we had been playing, all unawares, on the beach. It must have been a horrible shock for the poor woman finding her husband lying there.

"Everyone said it was Indian Tom who did it in revenge for an insult. Anyway, it was him they hanged although it took two trials and three years to do it. Mrs. Swan married a Portuguese fellow and they moved up to the coal mines at Nanaimo. I never did see Annie again after that day." Emily lapsed back into silence.

"But can't you find out now," asked Ian hesitantly.

"What do you mean?" Emily looked up puzzled. "Find out what?"

"Well," continued Ian uncertainly, "if it really was Indian Tom killed Mr. Swan. After all, you're all ghosts now, can't you ask him?"

There was a long silence during which the ghosts looked slightly confused. Ian was worried that he had offended them by referring to their status. At length it was Billy who broke the silence with a laugh.

"It doesn't seem to work that way," he said cheerily, "I cannot remember anything other than what happened in my life, so that will have to do."

He turned to Emily.

"But what I do remember, I remember very well. For example, I remember the day I was down beachcombing for logs on Pender Island. Must have been in the eighties sometime, anyway, I met this young lady, just sitting on a log doing needlepoint. Well what was I to do? I stopped and struck up a conversation. Her name was Margaret and she lived on the island with her sisters and her tyrannical mother. Now her mother had sworn that her precious daughters would never marry and she was so fearsome a creature that few young men ever ventured near the house. Margaret and I got around it by meeting on the beach in secret.

"Margaret was the oldest of the girls and had once almost escaped the old woman. She had persuaded her mother that it would be ladylike to take lessons from an artist over on Mayne. Each week she rowed across. The mother was very happy with all the pleasant sketches of flowers and driftwood that Margaret brought home. But one week she was over on the island getting supplies and decided to see for herself. She walked into the studio unannounced, and there was Margaret, the artist and three or four other students busily drawing the almost nude form of one of the Pritchett girls.

"Well, to Margaret's mother, artists' models were but one very small step away from ladies of the street and she was horrified at her daughter consorting with that sort. Margaret was dragged home and it was needlepoint under the mother's eagle eye for all of them from that moment on."

Ian smiled to himself. At last here was someone in all these stories who was as restricted as he was. He felt a wave of sympathy for poor Margaret trapped on the island. At least he wasn't forced to do needlepoint.

"At length, Margaret and I decided to marry, but I didn't have the courage to face the battle-axe, so we settled on elopement. Margaret packed a suitcase and hid it in the boathouse. One afternoon, while her mother and sisters were at pianoforte practice in the parlour, Margaret snuck away, collected her things and met me on the beach. But the mother was canny. She knew something was up and came looking. She burst through the trees just as I was helping Margaret into the boat. I don't think I've ever worked so fast in my life, throwing the suitcase in and pushing that boat off. We made it and I'll always remember the mother, standing with her black widow's skirts spread out in the water, screaming, 'Bring my daughter back, you wastrel,' and shaking her fist in the air. I just blew her a kiss and shouted back, 'Thank you for your blessings, mother.'"

Ian's sympathy for Margaret evaporated. Even she had escaped.

"We were married the day after we eloped. I thought Margaret's mother would calm down after she saw we were serious and there was nothing she could do, but she never did forgive us. Eventually, we had to move to Australia to escape."

"And I missed you ever after," said Emily looking at her brother who was fading rapidly. "He was always one to follow his heart," Emily added wistfully before lapsing into a silence which dragged on as the waves splashed against the wooden hull. Ian bailed some more. Eventually, he felt he had to say something.

"You had other brothers too?" he prompted.

Emily looked up sadly.

"Yes," she said, "two, but they both died. Donald was born when I was six and he became the third of our crew. He was the smallest and it always seemed he was running to try and keep up with Billy and me. He went into the logging and was killed in an accident over on the mainland in '96. Never even got the chance to marry."

"Was that who my grandfather was named after?" Ian asked.

"Yes," replied Emily, "he was my only son and he was born just four years after Donald was killed." She sat silent for a moment. When she continued talking, it was someone else who was on her mind.

"My other brother was Richard. He was an afterthought, born in '80 when I was already fifteen and only two years away from marrying myself. He was the loveliest baby and Billy was very cross at me because all I wanted to do was stay home and look after Richard while he wanted to be out hunting deer and grouse. I was very close to Richard, even after I married. He was close enough in age to my children that he used to come over and play with them."

"What happened?" Ian asked gently.

For the longest time Emily sat in silence. Eventually she looked up.

"I'll let him tell you," she said and faded. Her place was filled by a handsome man dressed in a quaint uniform. It consisted of heavy boots, long socks, a kilt and a short khaki jacket covered with brass buttons. The man wore a folding hat with a badge on the front and a dark tassel down the back.

Ian recognized the man immediately. He could picture a faded, leather-framed, sepia print of a young man in the same kilt and uniform standing formally in front of a studio backdrop and gazing confidently into the camera. The photograph sat on top of the piano in the spare room in Vancouver. Ian gasped. The man smiled.

"Hello," he said, "my name's Richard."

# Chapter Eight

"I'm Ian," Ian replied.

"Yes, I know," Richard continued. "Emily asked me to come here and tell you a story. It is not an easy story. There is tragedy in it and many sad things which happened in a different world long ago. Do you wish to hear it?"

Ian nodded.

"Very well then. As Emily said, I grew up on the island. I married Sarah in the year your grandfather Donald was born. Sarah was from an old English family that lived on Saturna and we had a good life. My only regret was that we could have no children, but we were happy in each other's company.

"The farm did well and I paid little attention to the larger world outside. But the outside world went on. Countries were building empires and fleets of steel battleships. And they were signing treaties with each other — treaties which would soon pull them all into a nightmare so large that even my little farm could not escape.

"The summer of 1914 was one of the most beautiful I could remember. Day after day the sun shone. We had good water so the plants and animals thrived. I could not have asked for more, but there must have been something more I wanted. Perhaps it was not having children to fill my spare time, but that endless summer I began to take an interest in the world outside. As the countries of Europe slipped towards war, I read everything I could find on politics; it became almost an obsession. Sarah could not understand my sudden interest, but she accepted that I had to try and make sense of what was going on.

"By the time war did break out in August, I had decided that the Kaiser in Germany was the one to blame. When he hurled his armies against France and Britain I was angry and determined that he had to be stopped. In that I was not alone and young men everywhere were flocking to join the army, their only concern that the fighting would be over before they were sent overseas.

"I decided to join up. Sarah and Emily both tried to dissuade me, but I was firm. I felt I had to do my bit and not skulk on my comfortable piece of land while others did the work. In any case, the general opinion was that the war would be over by Christmas and I thought I would surely be back in time to tend the crops next summer.

"Most of the boys were joining the local outfits, the Princess Patricia's or the Royal Canadian Regiment. I figured that I would be more use more quickly if I made my own way over to Britain and joined up there. I took the train out east and got on a ship bound for Europe. When I landed in Glasgow on the west coast of Scotland I went into the first recruiting office I could find and signed up. It was the Queen's Own Cameron Highlanders. They were already over in France fighting to stop the German advance at the Aisne and around Ypres but they were recruiting as fast as they could to replace the heavy casualties they suffered.

"I signed up and three days later I was getting my photograph taken in my new uniform. I felt about ten feet tall. I didn't even mind that the other recruits were calling me grandpa because I had reached the ripe old age of thirty-four. Most of them were only eighteen or twenty.

"We went into barracks in Scotland for training. It was boring, marching up and down Scottish byways in the cold rain of winter to no apparent purpose, but we counted ourselves lucky. So many had volunteered that a lot had no uniforms and had to train with wooden rifles. I could shoot quite well already, but some of the boys hardly knew which end of a rifle was which. Still, we learned how to march and how to drill, and how to care for our kit, and how to dig. We spent days digging trenches all over the Scottish landscape in all sorts of weather. And we developed a pride in being Camerons. The Camerons had stopped the Kaiser's Prussian

Guards outside Ypres, and probably saved the whole front in 1914 — so we had a proud past.

"Of course the Canadians were involved too. The Expeditionary Force was caught up in the first German poisoned gas attack in April of 1915 at Ypres. Suffered badly there too. And the Princess Patricia's, they got their first taste of war at Ypres in the spring. So my guess had been wrong, I had not got into action before my friends who had joined a local outfit.

"At last a group of us were sent over to France where we joined the regiment in August and began to prepare for the big attack on the 25th of September. We spent a lot of time training on a scale model of the front which was supposed to give us an idea of what the landscape would be like once we broke through the German lines. On the 21st of September the guns began firing. What a racket they made. One old soldier said he heard more guns in one hour than he had heard in the whole Boer War. To us new recruits it seemed as if there was a continuous train of solid steel and explosives being hurled over our heads at the Germans. The sound was like the end of the world. How could any of the enemy survive such a pasting? We were excited and raring to be going over the top. Some of the old soldiers were not so sure. They would cock an ear to the guns and shake their heads, claiming that from the sound of it a lot of the shells were duds which failed to explode. But we were all in high spirits and felt that once we started marching we wouldn't stop until we reached Berlin."

There they were again, Ian's ancestors marching off to adventure — gold rushes, wars — why was Ian's world so boring? There was no adventure for him to run off to.

"Trouble was, everyone knew that something big was going to happen — even the Germans. At one place they held up a huge sign which said, 'Why wait for the 25th, Jock, come on over now.' And they were dead right. It was supposed to be a big surprise. The main attack was at a place called Loos, up close to the Belgian border. The problem was a lot of new trenches had to be dug to hold all the soldiers for the attack and the ground was white chalk. So, every time a hole was dug it left a white pile of dirt on the ground. The Germans could see where all the digging was going on and figured that that was where the attack would come.

"Loos was a miserable place at the best of times. The land was as flat as Saskatchewan and the horizon was broken only by coal tips, pitheads and depressing clusters of miners' cottages. Out in front of our trenches the first thing you saw was the twin towers of the pithead at Loos itself. The English called it Tower Bridge after the bridge in London that it resembled. You could see it from everywhere on our front, and of course the Germans sitting on top of it could watch us dig all our new trenches.

"We were all given three days rest before the attack. They marched us back into the line on the 24th of September. It was a Friday and I remember the chill that went through me as we marched past a large pile of brand new coffins and a stack of fresh wooden crosses, neatly laid out beside a deep hole in the ground. Still, we all kept our high spirits. That night there were sing-songs and gambling all along the line. It was considered bad luck for a soldier to go into battle with money in his pocket and many seemed determined to lose all their pay that night.

"The guns kept at it all night and a thunderstorm added to the spectacle. We all had full equipment, two days rations, two extra bandoliers of ammunition and a shovel. The Camerons had one extra thing. All the divisions in the attack had coloured flags. We were to raise them when we achieved our objectives. One of our Sergeants had taken a piece of Cameron tartan and sewed it onto our flag, so we had our own regimental colours to take into battle, just like in the days of Napoleon and Wellington.

"We were all so crammed into the trenches that it was impossible to move and by midnight it was raining so hard that we were all soaked through. No one slept and we were all pretty tired and miserable by dawn.

"Just before it got light, all the other troops received their shot of rum. We didn't because our Colonel reckoned that if his soldiers were going to meet their maker that day, they should do it sober. It wasn't a bother to me, not being a great drinker, but some of the boys were more mad at the Colonel than at the Germans."

Richard looked up at Ian and smiled weakly. Reaching up he removed his cap and ran his fingers through his hair. Ian said nothing, not wanting to disturb the flow of the story.

It seemed to him that Richard was gathering his strength to continue. At length he went on.

"Loos was to be the first big use of poisoned gas. There were canisters and pipes all over the place. It was supposed to subdue the Germans who had survived the shelling so that we could just walk through. Trouble was, for gas to work, you need a wind and there was precious little of that on the 25th. In some places it even blew the wrong way and the gas poisoned our own soldiers.

"At last 6:30 a.m. came. The officers blew whistles and we all clambered up the ladders out into the open. It felt strange to be standing up after all the weeks of living underground. The gas was blowing on ahead of us in a grey-greenish cloud. Some of the officers had footballs. I heard one say, "Come on lads, I'll buy a drink for the man who kicks the ball into the German trench." Being a Scottish regiment, we had pipers leading us forward. Those men were the bravest I knew. The had to stand upright and walk toward the enemy trenches with no weapons, only their precious bag-pipes. The sound was supposed to scare the enemy. I don't know if it did, but it certainly raised our spirits to have these men playing us forward.

"Big guns were firing all around. Even so, it was strangely quiet after the days of barrage. After a year of war the ground was still covered with grass and there were still leaves on a few scattered trees. I was surprised to hear a bird singing in a lull.

"The Germans were firing their machine guns at us but it was through the gas and smoke so their aim was bad. Still, men were being hit. They would just gasp and lie down as if they were having a rest. My pal Frank, a prairie boy from Edmonton, was beside me. We had agreed to stay close so we could help each other if we got into trouble.

"Frank and I headed forward as fast as we could with all our equipment weighing us down. The wire in front of the German trenches was cut so we got into their front line quickly. The gas was still lying there and I got a whiff or two, but it had really demoralized the enemy. The few soldiers left were scared and disoriented and didn't put up too much resistance when they saw us charging down at them.

"Then we were in open country. The gas cleared and we could see German soldiers retreating back towards Tower Bridge and the village of Loos. We ran after them and by 9 a.m. we were in the streets of the town itself. We threw bombs down into the cellars to clear the Germans out. But we had to be careful because there were still some civilians in the town. I saw an old woman pushing a pram loaded with a mattress through all the fighting. She didn't even seem to notice the bullets chipping the wall above her head.

"When we got through Loos we formed up and advanced on Hill 70, the highest point of land around. We thought we had won. It was as if we were a holiday crowd at the seaside. All the boys took out cigarettes and a couple began playing mouth organs. We streamed up that hill — a magnificent rabble — champions of the world. We got to the top and raised our flag. It was a grand sight to see it fluttering in the breeze. We had lost a lot of men to the machine guns around Loos. I had a bullet hole in my sleeve and one through my pack and Frank was bleeding from a bullet that had nicked his ear. But we had won. We could see the Germans fleeing down the far side of the hill."

Richard paused again to gather himself for the finale of the tale.

"Then we made our big mistake," he continued quietly. "We followed the retreating Germans. We thought they were beaten, but they weren't. We had only got through their first line. We should have stayed where we were or gone straight ahead where the defenses were weak. Instead we streamed to the right, down the hill after the enemy — straight at the town of Lens and its unbroken wire and machine guns.

"When the machine guns opened up, men began falling in clumps. Then the heavy guns opened and shells began exploding all around us throwing dirt and hot pieces of metal all over. We couldn't go on. I wanted so desperately to lie down, dig myself into the ground if I could, but I couldn't. Frank kept running and we had to stay together. The last thing I remember is trying to catch him and opening my mouth to shout.

"That's the end." Richard looked straight into Ian's eyes. With an almost apologetic smile, he gradually faded to nothing.

Ian gazed for a long minute at the space where Richard had been. The adventure hadn't turned out to be so much fun after all. How would Ian's dreams end? Ian felt as if he had lost a friend. All Richard's hopes and dreams had ended in that one moment. What had happened? He had to know.

"What happened?" Ian wondered aloud.

"Frank survived the war." Emily was back, speaking quietly. "He came to visit us after it. Said he remembered that day at Loos. They were running together when a shell exploded nearby. He turned to tell Richard they should lie down — and he wasn't there.

"At first he thought Richard had fallen into a shell hole and he went back to look for him, but there was no sign anywhere. It must have been a direct hit — there was nothing left of poor Richard to find. I suppose that happened to a lot of young men in those days."

Emily fell silent. Even through his own misery, Ian was stunned by the tragic tale. Then he remembered something.

"The photograph," he said breaking into Emily's thoughts. "Mom has Richard's photograph. It sits on the piano in the spare room in Vancouver."

"Yes," said Emily, "he was very proud of that photograph. It was taken in Glasgow when he joined up and got his uniform. He sent a copy back to me, and he wrote on the back, 'To Emily — doesn't your baby brother look grand in his new uniform?'"

# Chapter Nine

Ian was so engrossed in Emily's story that he failed to notice that the boat was wallowing awkwardly in the wave troughs. Even the cold water slopping around his ankles didn't distract him. He listened intently as Emily continued. "I had just turned seventeen when I married Charlie. It wasn't an arranged marriage, but I didn't have a lot of say either. It just seemed that everyone thought it was a good idea and, eventually, Charlie and I did too.

"Charlie was ten years older than me. He had come up from California to look for gold and ended up working farms all over the islands. Eventually, he pre-empted the 100 acres beside ours and began working for himself. The year we were married, father got a job as lighthouse keeper so Charlie moved over into our place and we ran both parcels of land from there. We started out raising sheep and selling the lambs at the New Westminster market. We managed to keep most of the cougars away from the lambs in the spring and, by the second year had saved enough money to buy a cow. I called her Estella after Pip's love in Mr. Dickens' *Great Expectations*. That was my favourite book.

"Not that we made a lot of money farming in those early years, Charlie always had to go fishing or building to make ends meet, but we managed and the kids always had warm clothes and enough food. In fact, in a good year we were quite well off."

"Yeah," an accented voice joined Emily's, "especially that year my partners and I caught those seven thousand salmon in the Fraser River. That year they sold for four cents each. That was enough to buy us the lumber for a barn."

Another figure was materializing beside Emily. It was a wiry middle-aged man, dressed in a coarse work shirt and baggy pants held up by wide suspenders. His face was thin and a pair of blue eyes sparkled on either side of a pronounced nose. He wore a cloth cap tilted to one side of his head.

"Yes," Emily responded to the newcomer's statement, "but the next year the run was bad and you never went back after that." She turned to address Ian. "Ian, meet your great grandfather Charlie."

The pair nodded at each other. "Hello," was all Ian could think of to say.

"Hi," the ghost responded. "I think, young man, now that you have guests, you had best be doing some more bailing so as not to get their feet wet."

Ian looked down. There were five or six inches of water slopping around in the boat. He searched for the bailer. It had floated behind him. Awkwardly, he reached back and retrieved it. The whole operation seemed to take forever and the effort of bailing the water loomed before him like a mountain. The ghosts had begun talking again. Ian emptied one bailer full over the gunwales and listened. They were talking as much to each other as to him.

Odd, he reflected as he half listened. His ancestors had all had lots of adventures, but there was another side to their lives too. Most seemed to be married by the time they were Ian's age. Ian had no wish to be married. He wished desperately that he had a girlfriend, but not a wife. Marriage seemed to make people so boring. Married people never did anything exciting. What was the point of escaping to adventure if it just led to marriage and boredom?

"Ah, it was hard work," Charlie commented as if reading Ian's thoughts, "but you had to be able to turn your hand to anything to make ends meet. Take me for instance, I could fish, hunt, farm, beachcomb, and build roads as well as the next man. If the fish weren't running, I could do whatever was needed. I sold deer skins and ducks to the Victoria Chinese, and dogfish livers to the loggers over at New Westminster. Flexibility, that was the key . . ."

"Dogfish livers?" Ian interrupted.

"Yeah," said Charlie, smiling, "dogfish livers. Could fetch 25 or 30 cents a gallon if I was lucky."

"What did the loggers want dogfish livers for?"

"Well, there were some fellows claimed that eating them raw kept them regular and prevented all sorts of diseases, but I never met anyone who actually did eat them. Mostly they were rendered down for the oil, which stank real bad. The miners up at Extension and Union Bay used it in their lamps, but the loggers used most of it. They used to build skid roads to slide the big logs down hill to the mill or to the water. The road was made of logs, stripped of bark and imbedded in the ground. They were flattened on the top and the logs hauled over them by teams of oxen. They were beasts those bulls. Sixteen hundred pounds some of them and it could take ten or twelve to move some of the big logs. The bull whacker was the man who made it all work. A bad whacker could break a small operation. A good one would know each bull's name and talk to them, swear at them more often, individually. If his vocal persuasion didn't work, he always had the pole which had a barb on the end with which he could prod any beast that wasn't doing his bidding. It was a sight to see, I can tell you. A dozen of these beasts careening down the road with a log you could build a small village out of crashing along behind them." Charlie drifted off into silent reverie at the long forgotten vision.

"Oil?" Ian prompted at last.

"Oil? Oh yeah. The dogfish oil was smeared on the logs of the skid roads to make the logs run easier, give the bulls at least a fighting chance. Anyway, as I was saying, flexibility was the key for a man to make a go of it in those days."

"And a woman too," Emily joined in.

"What?" Charlie's train of thought was broken by the interruption. "What flexibility did women need staying home all the time looking after the farm and the kids? Sure it was hard sometimes, with me being away month after month, but it was straightforward work."

"Straightforward was it?" Emily sounded quite annoyed. "Charlie Park, you never had the slightest idea what being alone on the farm was like. Oh, you worked hard when you were here, and you were always good at spotting the likely chance and getting work where others couldn't, but it always used to irk me something terrible when you would come home with a few dollars in your pocket and all those stories you had heard from the boys at this camp or that dock.

"Don't get me wrong," Emily continued before Charlie could get a word in, "I certainly appreciated those dollars. They are what kept us going a lot of years. And I'm not saying you didn't care for the kids and the farm as much as me. It's just there didn't seem to be a centre to your life as there was to mine. I was on the farm all the time, winter, spring, summer, fall, every year. Most I ever took away was three days to go over to the market in Victoria come harvest time. The farms, first the one you set up, then my old homestead after father went off to the lighthouse work, were my life every minute of every day of every year.

"When we were first married and I had little Becky to look after on top of all the farm work, and I was not yet twenty, I was scared almost out of my wits by the responsibility. There was the stock to keep from being eaten, the crops to keep growing, and the drunken miners from the old Point Comfort Hotel to keep clear of. You don't remember it all; your mind was full of the price of dogfish livers, but I do. I remember every blessed minute of it. I remember how, when the creek dried up in summer we had to use the rain barrels: first some water for drinking, then the clothes got washed, then the kids, then the floors, and last the poor old dog. That water was pretty black by the time it was thrown on the vegetables.

"I remember the cycle of the seasons year after year: spring, with the planting and the lambing; summer, with all the crops to be tended and the worry of whether the creek would dry up this year or not; fall, with all the picking, packing, and shipping to the market in Victoria; and winter, either stuck inside and getting on each other's nerves or out looking to the stock in some freak snowstorm."

"Now hold on," Charlie had regained some composure after the initial outburst from Emily. "Sure you remember it all. No one is saying that you don't, and I appreciated your hard work more than anyone. But the work was monotonous. The problems we faced there, and you faced alone when I was away, were the same every season. You needed strength and courage to face them, but flexibility was something I needed moving from job to job and being ready to take advantage of the least opportunity when it presented itself. I am put in mind of the time I made good money raising birds for the cockfights in the city. . . "

"Yes, and the time you had that harebrained scheme to herd sheep up to feed the miners in the Klondike. Some worked and some didn't. If they didn't you just moved on to the next scheme. Mostly I couldn't afford to fail.

"Remember that spring you went to work on the roads and left me with the lambing? Becky was no more than two or three so it must have been '85 or '86. We'd been busy bringing in the sheep and separating them by the tar marks on their coats. They were ready to lamb and we had to protect them from the cougars. It had been a hard winter and the cougars were hungry and lean. Many's the night I was out in the yard with a pitch torch to scare them away, but they were desperate.

"One afternoon I was in the kitchen and Becky was playing in the dirt out back with the rag doll I had sewed that winter. It was March and the first day there was truly any warmth in the sun. I don't know why, maybe something caught the corner of my eye, but I looked out the kitchen window. There was a deep shadow in the corner under the apple tree. I had to look twice to be sure, but crouching in the shadow watching Becky was an old skinny cougar.

"I screamed, and kept on screaming as I ran out of the door. No mangy cougar was going to stalk my child. I think I went a little mad, but not too mad not to think to grab the broom propped up by the door. Becky must have thought her mother had gone crazy, bursting out of the house, screaming and waving a corn broom over her head. She burst into floods of tears, but I scared that old cougar too. He ran off into the bush. I grabbed Becky and the pair of us just sat in the dirt in tears until we calmed down.

"Now that was flexibility. No time for a second chance. If I make the wrong decision, I lose my child."

"Yes, that was flexibility," Charlie was smiling broadly, "and remember I put the rifle by the back door after that."

"Sure I remember," Emily was smiling too, "but you know, Charlie, like I always told you, a frightened mother with a broom is more than a match for any cougar — or a man with a gun."

Despite his misery, Ian found himself smiling along with the two ghosts. He was enjoying their stories. They were about a very different time, but still about things he could relate to. Real things, not the perfect world his father was always going on about.

He was rudely interrupted by the boat tilting wildly over to his left. Flailing madly, he threw himself to the right to try and regain balance. Waves, larger than usual, were buffeting the boat broadside on. That was causing the water Ian should have bailed out to slosh violently from one side to the other. Six inches of water in the bottom of the boat didn't appear much, but it was a lot of gallons and each gallon weighed ten pounds. Throw that weight from side to side as was happening now, and the boat was in serious danger of capsizing.

Ian felt panic rising in him through the cold. He had a decision to make. He could grab for the oars and try to turn the boat into the waves to stop the rocking, or he could go for the bailer and try to get rid of the water that was causing the problem. Neither option seemed easy right now when it was all Ian could do to hold his position. He was mildly annoyed to see that the ghosts were having no trouble and were sitting serenely in the stern, rolling with the waves and regarding him calmly.

Ian decided on the oars, but he never got the chance to find out if that was the right decision. He had one oar clenched firmly in his right hand and was reaching for the other when a large wave hit the side of the boat. It tilted crazily. Ian watched in horror as the water rushed over to one side, pushing the gunwales down and allowing a flood of cold sea water over into the boat. He didn't even have time to try and use his weight to right the boat before he found himself immersed in the cold water of Georgia Strait.

Panic flooded Ian's body. He was completely submerged. He had no idea which way was up, and he had swallowed a large amount of water. He barely had time to think, "I'm drowning!" before his life jacket pushed him to the surface and his head bobbed above the water.

Ian gasped a lungful of air and thanked the heavens that

he hadn't been too stupid to put on his life jacket. The large waves seemed to have passed, but the water was still choppy enough to confine Ian's world to a very small area of water and wind-blown spray. Outside that was complete darkness. There was no sign of the boat.

Oddly, Ian had completely stopped shivering and felt almost calm. The only sensation was a pain where the salt water was irritating the cut on his hand. Well, they'd be unlikely to find him now, a solitary head lost in the waves. It was a shame really.

Ian floated almost happily in the dark. Time slowed. This was peaceful and relaxing. Then a voice interrupted Ian's reverie.

"Hello! Over here," it said.

With almost glacial slowness, Ian turned towards the voice. He was looking for a rescue zodiac or a fishing boat. What he saw made him groan. The voice belonged to his great grandmother Emily. She and Charlie were still sitting, apparently comfortably, on the curving, overturned hull of Ian's rowboat. The bow, where the leak was, was low in the water, but the stern was high enough to be above the waves.

"I think you had better come over here and get out of the water," suggested Charlie. Weakly, Ian began kicking his legs.

"That's it. Come on," Emily encouraged him.

It seemed to take an age, but finally, Ian bumped against the upturned hull. The effort of pulling himself up the sloping wood seemed impossible. Maybe he could just float here, holding on. But Emily wouldn't let him rest.

"Come on," she shouted to him. "Just pull yourself up and you'll be a lot more comfortable. Besides, I haven't finished telling you stories."

With painful slowness, Ian struggled to haul himself out of the water. He had to be careful to keep the boat stable, but with Emily and Charlie's voices helping him, and using his last ounces of strength, he at last found himself out of the water and balanced precariously on the hull. Lying along the keel, with one leg and one arm on either side, he felt nearly as comfortable as he had floating in the water. With Emily's voice in his ear, congratulating him, he drifted off to sleep.

# Chapter Ten

"Best not to sleep, you might slip off into the water again." Charlie's voice was still bugging Ian through his drowsy numbness. He knew the ghost was right, he mustn't sleep. If he ended up in the water again, there was no way he would ever have the strength the pull himself out once more. But the urge to sleep was becoming overpowering, and he was cold. Colder than he had been in the water. The shivering had started again too. In fact, it was the shivering that eventually prevented Ian going to sleep and persuaded him to raise his head and address the source of the annoying voice.

"Stop bugging me," he said unkindly. "Why don't you go back to wherever it is you come from and leave me alone?"

The ghosts appeared to take no offense.

"I'm afraid I don't seem to have complete say in that," said Charlie. "In any case, I think you need us, and Emily here has more things to tell you."

"I don't want to hear any more dumb stories." Ian was feeling more lively the angrier he got. "Besides, it was you that got me into this mess. If you two hadn't distracted me with those stories, I would have been able to bail and the boat would never have swamped."

"Maybe so," Emily shrugged philosophically, "but if we hadn't persuaded you to climb onto the upturned boat, you'd still be floating around out there unconscious and probably dying. So I figure we might be even."

Ian grunted with ill-nature.

"Besides," Charlie added, "Emily knows how cold these waters are." He turned to his companion. "Remember the time you fell in on the way over to New Westminster?"

"Yes," replied Emily, "it was the only time I ever went over there, and it was you persuaded me to go." Charlie shrugged good-naturedly.

"Before they built the new wharf in Miner's Bay in December '85," Emily went on addressing Ian, "the big ships had to anchor out in the Pass and passengers rowed out to board them.

"Charlie was going over to talk to some business people about one of his schemes and decided to take me with him. We'd had a good year and Charlie said I could buy myself some material for a new dress. I . . . "

"Always was generous," interrupted Charlie with a smile.

"Oh yes," Emily responded, "generous to a fault if there was something in it for you. Now stop interrupting. Where was I? Oh yes, going over to New Westminster. I . . . "

"Why New Westminster? Wasn't Vancouver closer?" Ian was being drawn in again and couldn't help croaking the question. Emily didn't seem to mind his interruption.

"It would have been if it had existed then. Vancouver wasn't a city until '86, and then it burned to the ground in forty minutes, two month's later. New Westminster was the first city on the mainland. Of course, even when it was the capital, it never had the glitter or prestige, or even the size, of Victoria, but it was somewhere different and, in those days, I still had dreams of going to far away and exotic places," Emily glanced at Charlie who smiled but remained silent.

"New Westminster was hardly exotic," she continued addressing Ian, "but it was a start.

"The steamer I was to catch was the *Princess Louise*. She was my favourite. I used to love watching her go through at night, all lit up. I would imagine I was a princess on board. It was a choppy night and the row out towards the *Louise's* lights was rough. We were all experienced with boats, but coming up to a large ship was always dangerous. You had to be very careful to avoid the big side paddles and judge the rise and fall of the boats carefully. Just the year before a poor woman and her child had fallen in while boarding and drowned. Her skirts had pulled them both straight down. It was three days before the bodies were washed up on the beach.

"But I wasn't thinking about that. I was excited at going somewhere new. New Westminster had a bit of a reputation for being wilder than Victoria. Not that I was looking for the wild life, but it added a sense of excitement to the trip.

"Well, we got alongside the *Louise* without any problem and my bag was passed up. I was stepping onto the ladder that ran down the side of the big ship when the rowboat dropped and twisted away on a wave. All of a sudden, there was nothing below me but cold, dark water. As I went under, all I could think of besides the shock of the cold, were long black hands under the water scrabbling to catch hold of my skirts and pull me under. I thrashed about something fierce. Even knocked the hat off the boatman who eventually hauled me out.

"It was a wet and miserable beginning to my trip and I never did go back after that, even when the ferries began to dock in the bay and you could just walk on up the gangplank. The mainland wasn't for me — too dirty and noisy. I suppose I come from island stock and it's in my blood to want to be surrounded by water. Anyway, that was the only time I was in the water without wanting to be. It was a much shorter time than you, but it frightened me and showed me how quickly things can go wrong."

"Especially," Charlie added, "on boats, as you have found

out. But you have a choice. Boats to us were essential. There were precious few roads and no one island had everything a person needed. You had to row or sail to get the mail, or supplies, or spare parts for machinery, or stock, or to take produce to market. We would think nothing of rowing 10 or 12 miles in the morning and back at dusk. Boats were a part of our lives," he turned to Emily, "especially the life of old Neptune Grimmer." Emily nodded and Charlie continued. "His mother lived on Pender, but there was no midwife there so, when her time came due, her brother rowed her over to Mayne. But they were too slow. Nep came bawling into the world in the bottom of a rowboat in the middle of Navy Channel. Hence the name.

"Did you know that the *Tilikum* was built on Galiano?"

"What's the *Tilikum?*" Ian asked.

"The lad's never heard of the *Tilikum,*" shouted Charlie in mock horror, "why she was nothing more than the most famous vessel around here. Circumnavigated the globe she did, and started out as a Nootka dugout canoe."

"A dugout canoe that sailed around the world!" Ian was incredulous.

"Sure. Some of those things were huge, could carry dozens of men or hundreds of pounds of supplies. A lot of the early settlers bought them.

"Of course, the *Tilikum* was modified. Voss bought her and added decking and water-tight bulkheads, a keel, a cabin and three masts. She looked odd sailing up and down the coast, but she must have been seaworthy to sail as far as she did." Charlie lapsed again into reflection before continuing.

"Then there was the time the lighthouse keeper on Denman — what was his name?"

"Percy or Piercy, something like that," Emily answered.

"Piercy. That's right. He had ten kids living on a bare rock off the island. One day his eight-year-old boy, Harvey, found a blasting cap left over by the construction crew. He was playing with it and the thing went off, damn near took his hand. Anyway, his Dad rowed him over to the island, but keepers were under strict orders never to leave their lights for long. So Harvey found himself on the beach with a bandaged hand and directions for the six mile walk to the doctor's house." Charlie lapsed into silence.

"What happened to him?" Ian asked eventually.

"Who? Oh, young Harvey. He was fine. Doctor tended to him and took him over to Cumberland hospital. Folks were tough in those days, kid."

"Away with you Charlie," Emily joined in, "it wasn't toughness. We just made do, and we were flexible. Pretty quickly we learned what we needed to know and made what we couldn't afford or did without. But there was most of what we needed right to hand. Clearing the fields gave us wood for lumber, shakes, furniture, boats, sleds; the sheep supplied skins for mats, blankets and furniture upholstery and the wool to be carded, spun and woven into clothing;

and the deer and cattle gave us tanned hides, meat and fat for soap, candles and to grease machinery. Self-sufficiency, that was the key."

Teenagers are flexible reflected Ian. They had a lot of pressures — pressure to be academically successful without being a nerd; to wear cool clothes that your parents approved of enough to buy; to be popular with the guys and the girls. It was impossible. There was no way to satisfy everyone. On top of all that, Ian had his father's restrictions on where he spent his summers. Ian could tell Charlie and Emily about flexibility. If only he were allowed the self-sufficiency that his ancestors had.

"And we still had spare time for the finer things of life," Emily continued. "We had some splendid musical evenings with tenor voices and piano, banjo, guitar, violin and accordion accompaniment. It was hardly the Paris opera, but it served."

"You're right Emily, as usual," Charlie conceded happily. "Tell the lad about Harry Bullock's social events."

"Yes," Emily smiled at the memory. "Harry Bullock. He was one of the real characters. Built himself a twelve-room house and an English estate on Saltspring, just outside Ganges. Tried to bring England over to the wilds of the colonies. He used to have dinner parties and insisted that his guests were properly dressed. We were invited to one after Charlie did some work for him. We had to go, but Charlie was terrified."

"And no wonder," Charlie added, "black frock coat, bow tie and gloves. I had the devil's own job and my fair share of rude comments scrounging them from our rustic neighbours."

"The top hat was the best," Emily continued, "a size too small and perched on top of your head like a chimney flue." Both the ghosts laughed heartily at the memory.

"But you had it easy," continued Charlie at length, "old Bullock sent you over the gloves, a veil and earrings."

"It wasn't so easy," said Emily, "the nights I spent sewing my dress, and then having my ears pierced with a hot darning needle just to wear those earrings. Still, it was quite the occasion, almost thirty guests for a seven-course dinner. We had to eat at two sittings and Bullock sat and ate at both. Three pounds of meat at a serving. The man was prodigious."

"And he had an eye for the ladies too," Charlie added with a wink.

"Indeed," Emily agreed. "All the young, unattached social climbers were there with their corsets drawn in to give them the eighteen-inch waists and all wearing the same earrings as me. But for all his elegant pretensions, he was just as rough as us. Why, halfway through the meat course of our sitting, he puts down his knife, raises his fork and begins combing bits of food out of his beard with it."

"Yeah," Charlie laughed, "but we had all had so much to drink by then, I'm surprised anyone noticed."

"He was certainly liberal with his drink. It seems to me, you were so far gone you were barely able to find the boat, let alone row back home."

Ian groaned. No one had complained when Charlie got drunk. Ian was being punished just because he had been in the same room as people who had drunk too much. It was interesting that all these ancestors had come to tell Ian about the past, but the boy was beginning to wish for a time machine so that he could go back and live there. That would be freedom.

The pair sat in silence for a minute smiling over their memories. It was Charlie who began again.

"But sometimes people could be a little too self-sufficient," he said. "Like the time Peterson brought over drifters from Vancouver to vote for him in the elections. Picked two dozen of them up off the street, loaded them on his boat, sailed them over to vote at the hustings and paid each five dollars. He won the election, but he spent a year in prison for it."

"Didn't do him any harm in the long run," said Emily. "He ended up as Lieutenant-Governor."

"Yeah," agreed Charlie, "politics was fun in those days. Mind, so was smuggling. That started out as enterprising self-sufficiency, just not mentioning that you had bought some groceries on a trip to the San Juans. Everyone did it. Then some bright spark noticed that opium was selling for forty-five bucks in the States and only fifteen bucks in Canada. That was an opportunity too good to miss. Chinese used to bring it in on the big liners from Asia. Hide a bag in the coal for the voyage then drop it off the stern at a pre-arranged spot in the Strait for pickup.

"People too. For fifty bucks someone would smuggle a Chinese labourer over the border. 'Course, sometimes the cargo was dropped off on a beach inside Canada and told it was the States. I guess you had to be careful who you were dealing with.

"Wool was a big item too. Many's the farmer who used to leave bales in the barn at night and they would be gone in the morning, with a few dollars in their place. Burke was the one for that. Used to paint his boat black and row lying down with only his hat visible above the gunwales. Lots of folk did it. There was little harm."

"Until the liquor business started. That was more serious," Emily joined in.

"Yeah," agreed Charlie. "There was big business involved in that and a lot of money changed hands. Some of the big smuggling boats were fitted with airplane engines. They could do thirty-five or forty knots flat out — more than any of the Coast Guards. But they didn't have it all their own way; the Government boats had machine guns and were fitted with one-pounder cannons. Everyone carried a good stock of one inch doweling to plug the bullet holes. It's a wonder not more people were killed, although with all the rivalries, stories are that quite a few of the runners ended up at the bottom of the Strait on a dark night." Charlie gazed off to the side thoughtfully. "Those were good times," he eventually added wistfully. Then he began to fade.

Ian was sorry to see him go. He liked the cheerful American and his carefree view of the world. But now he was gone and Ian was left with Emily and the cold. Free of Charlie's stories, Ian's mind turned back to his predicament. He shivered violently, his teeth chattered noisily, and the upturned boat rocked.

"Emily I'm scared," he said.

# Chapter Eleven

"Now," Emily sounded forceful, "let's not be having any of that. People have been in much worse pickles than this and come out fine."

"I suppose," Ian said through his chattering teeth, "but what if they don't find me in time. . . " his voice trailed off to nothing.

"Of course they will," Emily certainly sounded confident. "We've got you out of the water and it's not long to sunup. Look, the sky is beginning to show some colour over there."

Ian turned his head and sure enough, there was a faint patch of watery paleness to the eastern sky.

"You're cold and wet and miserable, but you'll manage. Just like we all did in the old days."

"But not all of you did make it in the old days," Ian

pointed out, turning back to Emily. "What about Annie's father or the woman and child?"

"It was their time," said Emily gently. "I don't think it's yours yet."

"Do you know that for sure?" Ian lifted his head as high as he could and still maintain balance on the hull. Emily smiled.

"No," she said, "I don't know that for sure. It's just a feeling I have and I've always been right with my feelings. Your great great grandfather Ian said I had the second sight; that I could see the future. I never believed him. I always thought the second sight would mean you could see the details of what was going to happen, like watching a Charlie Chaplin movie, but maybe not. Maybe it is just a feeling about what is going to happen.

"I think many people, perhaps even most, have it in some form, but they ignore it. Bury the feeling under a blanket of rationalizations and tell themselves there's no such thing. If people let themselves go once in a while and acted on what they felt deep down inside, they might discover that they know more than they think they do."

"What happened to Charlie?" Ian asked in the silence that followed.

"Charlie? Charlie lived a long life. He saw many changes: steam replacing the oxen on the skid-roads and no more need for dogfish livers, engines replacing arms to move the boats between the islands, cars instead of buggies, law and order instead of lonely murders and gunboats firing into villages. He saw the island change from the rough and tumble place he knew into a settled, civilized place . . ."

"And a boring place," Charlie's voice echoed out of the darkness with a last word.

"Yes," agreed Emily smiling. "In some ways it was a more boring place, but it was safer and a better place to raise children. And Charlie adapted, however much he complained about missing the good old days. He still searched for adventure, even trying to join Richard in the Great War. That didn't last long. As soon as they discovered he was almost sixty they sent him home.

"We lived happily in the cabin with children and grandchildren around most of the time. One night in the fall of 1927, Charlie went to bed early. Said he was tired. The next morning I woke early and Charlie was there in the bed, dead, but with a lovely smile on his face. It was a heart attack, and I am sure he was dreaming of some crazy scheme when it happened.

"We buried him down at the little cemetery, and I bought the plot next to him. Thought it would only be few years before I joined him, but I hung around for another thirty-eight. Saw changes Charlie couldn't even dream about.

"But enough of that. I wanted to tell you about Cannon Paddon, and he would be fearful angry to hear me talking like some pagan mystic about second sight and dreams. He was the Anglican minister for the island from 1896 to 1922 and he was a real fire and brimstone man . . ."

"I was that," a rough Irish brogue joined, and then overwhelmed, Emily's voice. Emily faded to be replaced by a dark figure of an old man perched impossibly on the edge of the upturned boat. "I had to be, you see, to keep those mining boys in mind of the fear of the Lord. Most o' them was decent enough, just high-spirited after coming down from working their claims in the interior, but there was a few who spent more than their fair share of time in the lockup.

"Do you know what they used to call Mayne when I arrived?"

Ian shook his head.

"Little Hell. Imagine, me a minister in a place called Little Hell! I would have none o' that. I raised seven sons and two daughters. I raised them strict, but I raised them fair and they grew into fine young men and women. I treated the miners the same way. If they wished to go whooping it up in the old Point Comfort Hotel on Saturday night, I was there on Sunday morning to make sure they knew what the Lord thought o' their shenanigans.

"Young people in those days, and some older ones too, needed the fear of the Lord to keep them on the straight and narrow. Even the ones who thought they were holy, holy, needed reminding sometimes. There were many on the islands who were on the temperance side and felt that the Point Comfort should be closed down altogether. They were very loud about it, but I've seen some of them rowing over of a Saturday night to take a closer look at the old den of iniquity. It's not the temptations that need to be taken away, the devil will always find a way to place temptation in front of weak men and women, it's the spirit that needs to be strengthened. If people have a good healthy fear of the wrath o' the Lord, they'll surely think twice before indulging their baser cravings."

Surprisingly, the Cannon raised his head and winked broadly at Ian.

"Do you not think so, lad?" he asked.

Taking encouragement from the wink, Ian responded.

"Is it only fear of what will happen that keeps people doing the right thing?"

"No, no," the Cannon smiled, "but it helps. There are always people who know right from wrong and have no difficulty making their decisions and living with the consequences, and there are some who positively relish the pursuit of evil, but most are in the middle. Mostly they are decent, but they can be influenced and pushed to either side. It was my job to influence them in favour of the good, and fear of burning in hell was a mighty weapon in my armoury."

Ian's mind drifted to his own situation. He always seemed to know what was right. The trouble came when he tried to implement that, and a whole bunch of other factors — like not wanting to look like a dork in front of his classmates or having his emotions overwhelm all other sensations — came into play and made the whole situation unbearably complex. That was why Ian had gone to the party that his father was always reminding him about. It was considered cool to go, push limits, and take chances. Ian desperately wanted to be thought of as cool. But it had all gone wrong. Some of the kids had gone too far, drinking and smoking drugs. The parents had come home, the police had been called. Ian had been sober and straight, but that didn't make any difference with his father. He might as well have been discovered as high as a kite with a 26-ouncer in his hand.

"I found too that becoming something of a character also helped my cause," the Cannon's voice intruded into Ian's thoughts. "I designed a boat for travelling to visit my parishioners. It was quite a wondrous contraption, a rowboat without oars. I fitted it with side wheels which I turned with cranks. It was an experiment and it worked quite well in the calm but it was hard work in any kind of sea. I was going to scrap it when I heard people talking. They said how recognizable it was and how they had begun to associate the boat with me. Anything that kept me and my message in the forefront of my flock's minds was a good idea, so I kept it. Even added to it. When I was out at night I would keep a stable lantern lit beneath my cape. Apparently the glow was distinctive and could be seen for a considerable distance, so people knew I was out and about. It kept me in their minds you see, and had the added bonus of keeping my feet and legs warm while I went about God's work.

"God's work on the island was my life, at least after the accident. I was..."

"Accident?" Ian interrupted.

"Why, the Point Ellice Bridge collapse in Victoria in '96. A whole streetcar went down. Fifty-five people perished. I survived with only a few scrapes and bruises, but for ever after I had the sound of the poor souls screaming as the car went down locked in my head. They pulled me unconscious from the water and brought me to on the grass. The drowning wasn't too bad, quite relaxing in a way, but the resuscitation, now that was an ordeal I never wanted to go through again.

"After that I began thinking, why had I survived when so many had died? There must be a reason, and there was. There were plenty of ministers in Victoria, but the Lord's work was needed in Little Hell, so that is where I went for the rest of my days.

"It was hard work turning Little Hell into Little Heaven. We built the church from scratch. Problem was, we didn't have a font for baptizing the increasing number of babies. Eventually we found a naturally-hollowed sandstone basin on the beach. It took four strong men and a day's work to get it up to the church, but it served. I built a house and then watched it burn to the ground one night with everything I owned in it. But I never doubted for a moment that I was doing what I was intended to do. And I had the last laugh on the hell raisers. I left strict instructions that, when

I died, my funeral service should be held at five a.m. No one would get up that early just to be seen at a social occasion."

The Cannon lapsed into silence, faded and was replaced by Emily.

"Yes," she said quietly, "and you know, the church was packed that morning, hell-raising miners and all."

# Chapter Twelve

The rain had ceased and the sea, though still choppy, was calmer. The band of colour on the horizon was strengthening. Soon it would be light and the searchers would come. Ian hoped they would be in time. He was freezing, soaking and utterly exhausted. His mind alternated between periods of crystal lucidity and confused dullness. Time appeared to be passing with agonizing slowness, if at all. At least the ghosts, worrying as they might be for his sanity, had made the night pass quickly and, Ian had to admit, interestingly. The characters who had visited and the stories they had told had been varied and often entertaining enough to pull him out from his growing lethargy. And Emily was still here, sitting comfortably on the upturned boat. Maybe there was more yet to come. He should ask her. With immense effort, Ian lifted the front half of his body on his arms and attempted to sit up. It was a mistake. The hull, low in the water as it was, couldn't take the shift in weight. Abruptly it tipped over. Before he had time to react, Ian found himself back in the waters of Georgia Strait.

This time he panicked immediately. He was weak. He didn't have the strength left to haul himself back onto the hull. He wouldn't last long this time.

Flailing his arms and legs wildly, Ian only succeeded in swallowing more sea water. Against the brightening sky, Ian could just make out the silhouette of Emily, perched comfortably above the waves and watching him serenely.

"Help!" he croaked as he waved his arms and kicked his legs. Something brushed his ankle. Images of the waxen, seaweed-draped forms of the drowned woman and child pulling him down to a watery grave added impetus to his motions. He stubbed his toe painfully. Calmed and confused by the sudden shot of pain, Ian stopped waving his limbs around. His feet touched bottom and he found himself standing with water up to his chest. Waves still lifted him off his feet, but they always deposited him back gently on firm ground.

Turning his head, Ian saw a beach not twenty metres from where he stood. It was pebbly and sloped gently up to a line of white driftwood which bordered a dark mass of trees. Slightly embarrassed by his panic, Ian stumbled through the surf and collapsed amongst the rocks.

"You one very lucky boy," a strange voice close to his head said.

Rescue! Ian jerked his head up, but it was just another ghost. He knew immediately from the old fashioned clothes and the fact that he could just make out the line of driftwood through the character's waist. This one was Chinese. It was a man, dressed in a black, high-necked, collarless smock and loose trousers. The man's feet were visible through rough, rope sandals. Ian groaned between shivers.

"What do you want?" he asked wearily.

"I want nothing," the man replied cheerfully. "My name Lee and it no right you go thinking all people on islands white. There many nations here. Indians you know, but many more. Many black men on Saltspring."

"Yeah," interrupted Ian, "runaway slaves weren't they?"

"No," said Lee smiling. "Free men. Business men come from San Francisco. Come Victoria because no like anti-black laws in California. But much prejudice in Victoria too. So some go to islands to farm. No prejudice on islands then. Everyone accept everyone else. Anyone marry who they want, black, white, Indian, it no difference. Even Kanakas."

"Kanakas?" Ian asked.

"Yes. Yes." said Lee enthusiastically. "Many Kanakas."

"Who are Kanakas?" Ian interrupted hurriedly.

"Kanakas. Men from Sandwich Islands. Hudson's Bay men. Four hundred brought over to speak Indian. Very good at languages. Translate Indian for poor Scotchmen who not speak good English. Ha, ha."

Ian gazed in amazement at his exuberant companion.

"And Chinese?" he said at length.

"Yes," Lee agreed. "Many Chinese. This Gold Mountain for us. Make much money, bring family, but head tax very high, and work on roads, railways and mines very hard. Many die. My brother die in coal mine in Nanaimo. Big explosion. Kill many. Brother no name, Chinaman number 237, that all. I lucky. I work for Mrs. Emily when Mr. Charlie away. She very kind lady."

Lee's face clouded over and he looked glumly at the ground. It was such a radical change of expression for him, that Ian couldn't help asking what was wrong.

"Oh," responded Lee looking up again. "I not fair Mrs. Emily. I work many years. Very happy, but I have rice whisky still in woods. Not big, just a little for me and my family and a little to sell."

"You sold illegal liquor?"

"Not illegal in China," Lee said defensively. "Anyway, police catch me. Put in prison three year. Not fair to Mrs. Emily. Leave her without help. But I trick police." Lee brightened considerably. "Allowed one visitor every two weeks. My cousin live Victoria and he come visit me. We same size and, to white men, all Chinamen look same. So I say cousin, 'We change clothes. I go out, see family, maybe go Mah Yong house. Two weeks I come back we change back again.'"

Lee chuckled to himself at the memory. "My cousin, he want money, but okay. I have money in tin on shelf in Mrs. Emily's kitchen. I go get it, but Mrs. Emily hear me. I say, 'Sorry Mrs. Emily. Just me Lee. Get tin, go.' But I think I scare her pretty bad."

"You certainly did. Worst fright I ever got seeing you standing in my kitchen when you should have been in jail in Victoria." Emily materialized beside Lee. He looked over at her.

"Sorry, Mrs. Emily," he said, "but I pay cousin. Only do half time in prison. Ha, ha." His laughter echoed down the beach as he faded into nothingness.

"He was quite the character," Emily said cheerfully. "There was no shortage of characters on the islands and tremendous variety. Island people live long lives. And some say it is because of all the different genes, black, white, Indian, Chinese . . . "

"Lee talked about the. . . Kanakas," Ian interrupted.

"Yes," said Emily, "from the Sandwich Islands, what you call Hawaii now. They were good people. So were the Japanese. In the 1930s, one in every three islanders on Mayne was Japanese. They ran market gardens and fish canneries.

"I remember the Tanimoto family who lived just down the road from us. They grew the most beautiful tomatoes you have ever seen. Very conscientious farmers. Mr. Tanimoto had come over before the Great War to work in the canneries and the fisheries on the Fraser River. When the fishing season ended in the fall, he used to come over to Mayne to cut cordwood, clear land and work on the farms. Eventually, he saved enough money to buy some land and settle with his family.

"He started out exporting dried seaweed back to Japan, but then he went into growing tomatoes. The climate was sunnier on the islands so our tomatoes were ripe a full two weeks before the farms on the mainland.

"Mr. Tanimoto's children used to play with my grand-children all the time. Of course the second war changed everything. I'll never forget sitting in the cabin in silence around the radio listening to the announcement that the American base at Pearl Harbour had been bombed by the Japanese. That was December 7, 1941. The announcer had only just finished giving us the news when there was a knock on the door. It was Kiyoshi, Mr. Tanimoto's oldest boy. He was in tears. Apparently the RCMP had arrived and taken his father away. We thought there must have been some mistake, but there wasn't. They took three other island men away that night.

"The following year they came and took the rest of the family too. It was in April and almost all the island turned out on the dock to wish them well as they were herded onto the *Princess Mary* at Miner's Bay. There were a lot of tears that day.

"They moved the Tanimotos to southern Alberta. We had promised Mrs. Tanimoto that we would buy her husband's farm and hold it for them until they returned, but the gov-ernment made that illegal, said it was a criminal offense. I never did understand that. So much unnecessary heart-break and broken dreams and they wouldn't even let us do the minimum to help our friends. They said the land was to be kept for servicemen returning from the war, but no one ever bought the Tanimoto's greenhouses. They just became overgrown and wild.

"Those were difficult times all right. Many of the Japanese who were sent away had lived on the islands for two or three generations. They were as Canadian as the Scottish or Irish settlers. So many were sent away from Mayne that we had to close the school for shortage of children. It was so unfair. I heard a story of one Japanese man who pushed his very valuable grand piano off the end of the pier in Vancouver because he wasn't allowed to take it with him to the internment camp and he knew it would be stolen or sold for next to nothing if he left it. It was his only way to protest.

"The Tanimotos never did come back after 1945. They stayed in Alberta. They did send us a Christmas card every year until well into the '50's. The cards never gave much news, but every one had a location on the Tanimoto's farm handwritten on the back. Each year we would go out and dig at the location and uncover a bottle of Saki that old Mrs. Tanimoto had buried to save for their return. It was their thanks for trying to hold the place for them. Not much from their lives before the war, but at least we could toast their memory every year around the Christmas tree."

"The government apologized and gave compensation," Ian said remembering a news item he had seen a few years earlier, "but I don't suppose it did Mr. Tanimoto any good."

"No," agreed Emily, "but perhaps his children were

helped. The really sad thing was that it was a way of life that enriched the variety of the islands that was lost forever. That could never be brought back." She lapsed into silence and let her gaze drift over the water.

# Chapter Thirteen

The upturned boat had drifted in and was bumping softly against the rocks at the tide line. The sun was beginning to show over the horizon and it was almost fully light. The last of the rain clouds were being chased far to the west. It was going to be a warm day.

"They'll be out looking for me by now," Ian said. Emily nodded. With a tremendous effort, Ian hauled himself away from the water, turned over and propped his back against a log. He was still shivering and feeling cold, and he was having terrible difficulty organizing his thoughts into some kind of coherent order, but the first rays of the sun were hitting the beach now, sparkling on the water and painting the trees a rich golden colour. Their promise of warmth was good.

Emily's voice interrupted his reverie. "They'll be here soon," she said.

"Yes, they should be," agreed Ian. In a moment's silence, Ian thought back over all the characters he had met this night. Some he had never even dreamed existed, yet now he would never be able to forget them. But there was one more he still had to know about.

"Tell me about grandfather Donald?" he asked.

"I'll do better than that," replied Emily wistfully, "I'll tell you about all my children.

"Your great aunt Becky and the cougar you know about already. She was my first child. She married an Australian lad who had pre-empted land on Saltspring and, eventually, they moved back to his home. Settled close to Billy and had lots of children, so there must be a strong branch of the family down there still.

"Mary was the second, she was born in 1887. Married a miner and moved to Nanaimo. They never had any children but I was always thankful that they were close enough to visit me regularly.

"Two years after Mary there was Dorothy. She was my artistic child, always drawing or painting something. She went to art school and became quite accomplished. Worked in Victoria for ten years and made quite a name for herself painting coastal scenes. She was a great admirer of Lawren Harris and knew Emily Carr quite well. I think she would have been famous, but she caught the flu in the epidemic of

1919 and died at only thirty. I kept all her paintings. Maybe there are still some around."

Emily fell silent and thoughtful. Ian didn't want to interrupt her memories. At last she continued.

"Sadie was next. My little Sadie. She was born in '93 and surprised us all with her shock of bright red hair. And she had a temper to go with it. Always a handful, even as a baby." Emily paused as if gathering strength to go on.

"The winter of '96 was hard, one of the worst I can remember. Around the beginning of January Sadie caught a chill. Couldn't throw it off. Didn't worry us at first, children get chills, but the longer it dragged on the more worried I became. At the end of the month we had a big snowfall. Unusual, and it trapped us in the cabin for three days. In those three days Sadie became much worse. Ran a high fever and her lungs filled up so that she could hardly breathe. At last we cleared a way and got her to old doctor Nesbitt. But it was too late. She died the next day. Pneumonia it was.

"It took me a long time to stop blaming myself and Charlie for not forcing a way through those snow drifts and getting help sooner, even though Nesbitt said he doubted there was anything he could have done even if we had got her there earlier. No antibiotics in those days, you see.

"Life has to go on, and there were other children to care for. That was a hard year. In the summer news came that Donald had been killed in a logging accident. A pile of logs he was working on rolled and crushed him and another

man. The body was so disfigured they wouldn't even send
it home. It wasn't for another four years, until your grandfather Donald came along, that I felt I was close to normal
again.

"Donald was born in 1900, at the beginning of a new
century, full of hope and dreams. Right from the start he
was a feisty child, always in motion and always getting into
some mischief or other. I spent more time bandaging up his
cuts and sprains than I did with all my other children together. But he never learned. Didn't care about the pain I
suppose. Life was to be lived to the full and minor upsets
like injuries shouldn't be allowed to get in the way."

Ian was having trouble reconciling Emily's description of
the young tearaway Donald, with the old man he had briefly
known. This Donald sounded more like the guys who had
got Ian into trouble than one of his relatives. But he didn't
have long to reflect. A gruff voice broke into his thoughts.

"Damn right!" it said. "Life is for living."

Ian turned his head to see an almost-forgotten figure
striding towards him. Grandfather Donald had died when
Ian was only five, so it was through five-year-old eyes that
Ian remembered. But the memory was incredibly vivid. It
was the last time Ian had seen his grandpa.

The family had gone to the care facility where Donald
lived for the final few years of his life. The old man was
obviously sick. He sat in a chair beside his bed looking thin
and grey. Even the bright cheeriness of the room appeared

to have no effect on him. Ian could not believe that someone as old and wrinkled as his grandpa could still be alive,
but there he sat, his face surrounded by a shock of white
hair and beard and his watery eyes drifting aimlessly around
the room.

"Go and kiss your grandpa hello," Ian's father had said.
Ian had protested, but Jim had insisted. As he moved toward
the old man, Ian felt himself being slowly overwhelmed by
the stale smell of old age that not even the pine fresh anti-
septic of the room could conceal. Ian's gaze was held by an
area of white drool which nestled in the wrinkles by the old
man's mouth and matted the straggly beard hairs. The lips
were moving, but nothing understandable was coming out.

It took all Ian's courage to approach Donald and give
him the quickest of pecks on the cheek. Then he fled. The
rest of the visit, he spent gazing out the window, looking
out at the grounds where lonely figures with canes or in
wheelchairs were scattered around in the late afternoon sun
like debris after some long-forgotten battle. A few days later
word arrived that grandpa Donald had died in his sleep. Ian
felt a twinge of guilt as he remembered that his first reac-
tion to the news had been relief.

The figure approaching him now along the beach was
recognizable. The deep wrinkles, and the straggling white
hair and beard were familiar, but there was a spring in the
step and a sparkle in the eye that Ian had never seen in the
old man he had disliked as a child. Incongruously, the fig-

ure wore a stained, deep red dressing gown tied at the waist with an old tie. Pausing only to hawk and spit noisily onto the beach, grandpa Donald strode forward and seated himself on the log beside Ian.

"Life's to be lived at full speed, or it shouldn't be lived at all. That was what I found most difficult about getting old. I could no longer do the things I wanted. That's what made me resent you, boy."

"Resent me?" Ian was shocked. "You resented me? But I was only five."

"Exactly," said the old man, "five-years-old and just like me at that age. You had the world at your feet. You could do anything you wanted and your mind and body would obey you. There was I, not even able to keep myself clean and drooling like a helpless baby. I was disgusted at myself and I envied you the life you had to live."

Ian was amazed. The idea that the old man who had scared him so had actually envied him was new.

"You must have been terrified of me," Donald continued. "Sometimes I even felt ashamed that all an old man could do was scare a child. But there was nothing I could do about it. All I could do was sit and drool, and I hated it."

Ian could think of nothing to say to break the ensuing silence. He just sat against the log staring at the ghost, his mouth hanging open.

"Close your mouth boy," Donald warned him, "you'll catch flies if you leave it hanging open like that."

A smile crossed the old man's face and, for a moment,

Ian could see shades of his own father amidst the wrinkles and folds. Were they more alike in other ways too?

"Anyway," Donald continued hurriedly, "when I was your age now, I tried to join the army. Uncle Richard had gone off and I reckoned I could lie my way through. Damn nearly did too. I snuck away one time when we were all on a trip over to Victoria and went to the recruiting office. The sergeant asked me my age and I added two years on and said sixteen because that was what I thought you had to be. I was big for my age and probably looked it.

"The sergeant looked me up and down and said, "Go and take a walk around the harbour, son. Come back in half an hour when you're nineteen." It took me a moment to work out what he meant, but I did and a half hour later I was nineteen and signing the papers.

"Mother was angry when I proudly told her what I had done, but I don't think it was a complete surprise to her. She had brought my birth certificate with her in her bag. She hauled me all the way back to the recruiting office by the ear, and brandished the certificate in front of the sergeant. Made him tear up the papers right then and there. I think the army could have used a few of her.

"She kept a close eye on me after that, especially after we heard the news about Richard. Still, the day after I turned nineteen, I was back in the office and this time there was nothing mother could do about it. She wasn't happy, but my mind was made up and there was no changing it.

"I suppose, fortunately, although I didn't think so at the

time, the war ended before my training and I never did see action. Got over to Europe though and decided to stay for a bit to look around. It was an exciting time, revolution and war in Russia, revolution in Germany, kings and emperors falling all over the place and a feeling that there was real change in the air. Socialism and communism meant something then and we were all trying to make the world a better, fairer place. We wanted the working man to get a fair deal and not be enslaved by corrupt mine bosses or factory owners. We wrote pamphlets, we marched, we battled police on the streets. It was an exciting time.

"I travelled all over, working at anything I could turn my hand to, even spent a couple of years on a freighter in the China Seas. Got involved in the labour movement whenever I could and got my head broken by a police billy club more than once. I learned that the only person who will look out for you is yourself, and if you don't, you're lost. 'Course, that's not to say you shouldn't help others whenever you can. We're a cooperative species despite what the bosses try to tell us, but you can't rely on the authorities to help you or do what is best for you. They have their own agenda and if it's not the same as yours, guess who will be the one to suffer?" Donald smiled ruefully before continuing.

"It always amazed me, even years later after Stalin had destroyed all of communism's hopes with his camps and purges, how law-abiding Canadians are. Even in the De-

pression, when people had such an obvious right to criti-
cize the government and try to change it, they still went on
as if nothing were happening. I used to get into a lot of
trouble around here for speaking my mind. 'People show
far too much respect for authority,' I used to tell them.
'Those men in Victoria and Ottawa are there to work for us
and if we don't like what they do we should damn well
throw them out.'

"Well, no one listened, so I just got on with my own life
and running the farm. I came back after Charlie died. Had
to really, couldn't leave mother on her own, but I had had
enough of travelling by then. The more you travel, the more
you realize how much everywhere is the same. I was ready
to settle down for a while and give the farm a try. Some try.
I never left.

"Almost did once though," Donald continued. "It was in
'36 when the war broke out in Spain. Fascism was on the
rise everywhere, even in good old Canada. Black-shirted
thugs were smashing Jewish shop windows in Montreal and
the Prime Minister was shaking hands with Hitler and saying what a splendid fellow he was. It seemed as if it was only
a matter of time, and no one was doing anything about it.
When the Army revolted in Spain it seemed a glorious
opportunity to do something, by going to help the republi-
can government put down the revolt. Working men from
all over the world were flocking to Madrid. I nearly did."

Donald fell silent again.

"Why didn't you?" Ian asked. The old man smiled.

"I wasn't my own man anymore," he said. "I'd been married for two years by then, to Helen.

"Ah," Donald went on reflectively, "she was a lovely woman, quiet and with the most beautiful auburn hair I had ever seen."

"And with a mind that was at least the match of yours," interrupted Emily.

"Yes indeed," Donald laughed. "The nights we sat up to three or four in the morning thrashing out the world's problems. Helen came from one of the old families on Pender, and I don't think her parents ever really approved of me, but we were a perfect match. I think if I had gone to Spain, she would have come too. We both believed it was important, and she could have easily worked in a hospital or with an ambulance unit. But it was too late."

"Too late?" Ian asked.

"Yes, too late. Helen was pregnant by then and there was no way I was going to leave her or take her to a war."

"Dad," Ian said in momentary realization.

"Indeed," replied Donald. His voice had become very soft and Ian could swear he could see a tear in the old man's eye. "Jim was on the way." Donald paused to collect himself.

"Your father's birth was the happiest, and the saddest, moment in my life."

A faint clattering sound began to intrude into the story. Ian tried to shrug it off, but it was persistent. And it was getting louder. Ian looked up, squinting against the low sun. There, out in the Strait, was a large helicopter. It was flying in a pattern of lines, up, over and down, up over and down. "It's looking for me," Ian thought. Then another thought crossed his mind, "not yet. I'm not finished here." Forcing himself to look away from the helicopter, he returned his gaze to Donald who was still talking.

"I was delighted to have a son," the old man went on, oblivious to the distant rotor blades. "I never forgot the morning Jim arrived, all red and bawling. I held him in the crook of my arm and just gazed at his face. To see a new life that I was responsible for was thrilling and frightening all at once. I was truly happy." Another moment of silence overcame him. He lowered his eyes to the beach

"But it didn't last. There were complications with the birth and three days later Helen was dead. To go from such heights to such depths in so short a time — I almost gave up. But there was always Jim. He needed me and his existence kept me centred through my grief even though I don't think I ever recovered from the loss of Helen.

"Emily and I brought up your dad. I loved him more than life itself. He was all that I had left of Helen, but . . . "

The silence returned and, this time, lasted for long minutes. Donald was obviously struggling with something very difficult. A last he continued, slowly and with many hesitations.

"I loved him," he repeated, "but a tiny part of me couldn't

help blaming Jim in some way for Helen's death. I knew it wasn't fair, and I despised that part of me. I fought to never let it show, but it was there, and, sometimes, I think Jim knew it in some instinctive way.

"I suppose some bitterness began to creep into me after that. I tried hard to be fair, but I found myself less flexible the older I got. And Jim wasn't an easy child — always had a mind of his own. Like me, I suppose. We used to have the most violent rows, shouting and yelling at each other over things that really didn't seem that important after we had calmed down.

"When I was calm I used to tell myself: 'Stop this or you will make the boy hate you,' but I couldn't. We kept arguing. I guess we were just too much the same and too different.

"Things came to a head the time Jim ran away from home."

"Ran away from home!" Ian couldn't help himself. "Dad ran away from home?"

"Yes," Donald continued, "it was the summer of 1950, so he would have been your age exactly. Planned it in every detail. Said he was going fishing for the day but he jumped the ferry and left. Made it all the way to Seattle before the police picked him up a full week later and brought him home.

"He really scared me that time. I thought I would never see him again and that made me think how much I would miss him. It also made me think that he must hate me a lot to go to such lengths to escape."

Donald fell silent again.

"Anyway, Jim did leave eventually. He went off to do a degree in engineering at the university in Vancouver. It was probably a smart move, no future in farming, but it was hard having no one to take over the land Emily and I had put so much into over the years. I often wondered if I had driven him away with my damned guilt over Helen.

"But I was very proud of him. He did well, making his own way in the world," Donald laughed again, "just like I had done.

"My life wasn't bad. In fact it was very good by most standards. I got to see more of the world and life than most people do and, with Helen, I had a few years of the kind of happiness most men only dream of. If I have one regret, it is that Jim and I never resolved our differences before I died."

Donald lapsed into silence and faded into nothing. Ian sat watching Emily and thinking about the stories he had heard. Somehow the way his Dad reacted to him made more sense now that he knew his history. Perhaps it might be easier now he understood something about his grandfather. Maybe they could talk about it.

Ian realized another thing too. For all their apparent freedom to go to war or gold rushes, his ancestors had been just as trapped as he was — trapped by circumstances, by necessities of the moment, by their time. Freedom was not trying to escape — escape for its own sake led nowhere. Freedom was accepting who you were and where and when you lived, and still living your life to the full.

The helicopter was still quartering the ocean in the distance. Ian shivered despite the noticeable warmth of the early sun. "It'll take them forever to work their way in here at that rate," he thought. "I wonder if I could build a signal?"

Ian's thoughts were rudely interrupted by a much louder noise. He just had time to look up before a second helicopter burst around the point to the south. It was flying very low, following the beach and tilting from side to side to give the goggled observer good views of the water line. As it roared level, Ian stood and waved. A gloved hand in the machine's bubble waved back and pointed him out to the pilot. The helicopter swung around in a wide, low circle, the wind from its blades stirring the treetops and flattening the water.

"Good-bye," Ian thought he heard a voice above the racket of the helicopter's blades. Turning, he looked at the spot where Emily had stood. He thought he saw a flicker in the air, but the space was empty. He turned slowly and examined the beach all around him. It was empty apart from the upturned boat stranded by the now retreating tide.

"Good-bye," he said, as the helicopter swung around and descended towards the open beach.

# Chapter Fourteen

The roar inside the helicopter was deafening, but Ian didn't mind. He was wrapped in dry, warm blankets and strapped into the back seat beside the observer. He had almost stopped shivering.

" . . . on the beach?"

"What?" Ian asked. The observer had said something to him, but he had missed most of it beneath the noise of the engine.

"Who was that with you on the beach?" he repeated in Ian's ear. Ian felt himself go tense.

"What do you mean?" he asked stalling for time.

"Well," continued the observer, "when we first rounded the point, I scanned the whole beach quickly. I could have sworn I saw two figures. One sitting down, that would have been you, and one standing. The standing figure looked like an old lady. That made me think it wasn't you but a couple of early morning walkers, so I went back to looking at the beach below the chopper. It was only when we drew level with you that I saw the boat. I knew then it must be you, and then I saw you wave, but you were alone. Who was the other person and why did they run off so quickly?"

Ian's mind was a turmoil. Should he deny that anyone else was there and risk antagonizing this man who was, after all, trained to see exactly this sort of thing, or should he invent a meeting with someone who ran off and risk his story being checked? He certainly wasn't going to say anything about ghosts. Then they would have him in the hospital so fast his feet wouldn't touch the ground. Whatever he did, he had to do it quickly. What was the simplest solution?

"What other person?" he said as innocently as he could manage. "I never met anyone on the beach. What would an old lady be doing out here on her own anyway?"

The observer watched Ian for what seemed like an age.

"Yeah, well," he said at last, "it does seem unlikely. The low sun can play tricks with the shadows. I only got a glimpse. Perhaps it was a piece of driftwood after all."

Ian got the impression that the observer didn't completely believe him. The man continued to stare at him closely. But what could he do? If Ian stuck to his story, then people would think the observer was going crazy if he started talking about old women on the beach.

His thoughts were interrupted by the pilot waving to attract his attention and pointing out the window. Below them lay Sturdies Bay and Ian could make out the tall and short figures of his parents standing in front of a crowd of onlookers by the helipad. He waved through the window as the helicopter circled to land.

꙰

After all the embraces and tears were done, Ian was taken to the Harbourmaster's hut where he was given a hot drink and a sandwich and where a local doctor examined him and bandaged his cut hand. The doctor pronounced him in good condition, considering his recent ordeal.

At last the doctor left, leaving an exhausted Ian with his parents.

"They'll take us back over in a little while, and you can get some sleep," Jim said quietly. There was a silence in which no one seemed able to think of anything to say. Ian's father broke it.

"What made you do such a thing?" He didn't ask the question unkindly, but Ian felt himself become defensive nonetheless.

"I don't know," he shrugged, "I wanted to get over to Galiano."

"To worry us?" his father asked.

"No," Ian hesitated, "Yes, I suppose partly. I was angry after our fight and I wanted to show you that you couldn't force me to live on this island. I didn't realize how strong the current was."

"It was a dumb thing to do," his father interrupted almost aggressively.

Ian forced himself to swallow the anger he felt rising within him.

"I know that, Dad," he said as calmly as he could manage.

"Well, yes," his father continued, "I guess we all make mistakes now and then."

Ian only just managed to prevent his jaw dropping open. His father was backing off. His own anger vanished.

"It won't happen again," he said.

Jim looked up and smiled at his son.

"Peg, would you mind getting me a refill of coffee and maybe a hot chocolate for Ian?" He said looking over at his wife.

Ian shook his head. "Not for me thanks," he said.

Peg smiled and left the room. Ian watched his father carefully. He seemed almost nervous.

"Son, I . . . " he began hesitantly. Ian interrupted.

"Dad, no. There are a couple of things I want to say first. I wasn't trying to run away from home last night."

Jim was watching his son closely.

"Yes, I wanted to worry you, but more than that I wanted to prove I could make my own choices and decisions. It wasn't a great decision, but what was important was that it was mine. I always intended to come back today."

The pair looked at each other for a long moment. It was Jim who broke the silence.

"I ran away from home when I was your age. I mean really ran away from home — planned it and everything. I was going to head down to California and make it rich. Luckily I got picked up in Seattle and sent home." Jim laughed ruefully, "I guess the island was too small for me at that age too."

Ian smiled. "The other thing I wanted to say," he continued, "was that I did a lot of thinking last night. There wasn't much else to do, and some really weird things happened. Maybe I'll tell you about them one day, but I thought a lot about grandpa Donald. He used to scare the sh . . . He used to scare me a lot, but I guess that was just because he was old and I was just a little kid."

"No," Jim smiled ruefully, "he used to scare me a lot too. Even when I was a grown man."

"Anyway," Ian continued slowly, "It struck me that he must have been very like you when he was younger, and maybe that was why you two didn't get on so well."

"How did you know we didn't get on?"

"I guessed," Ian moved on quickly before his father pursued the question. "That time you left home, did you hate him?"

"Hate him?" Jim repeated thoughtfully. "No, I didn't hate him. There were times he almost drove me crazy and I resented his strictness, but I never hated him. The problem was within me. I felt so trapped sometimes it seemed like I was going to explode.

"It can't have been easy for him, bringing me up with only Emily to help. Sometimes I wondered if he ever blamed me for Helen's death."

"No he didn't," Ian blurted out. Jim looked at him carefully.

"I wish I could be certain," he said.

"I am," Ian continued. "I think, at the end, he wanted to tell you how much he loved you, but he was so set in his ways by then that he couldn't bring himself to say the words. And I think he was very proud of how well you did."

Jim was looking at his son with frank amazement.

"Do you think so?" he asked. "I always thought he hated the way I had abandoned the farm."

"That must have been hard for him," Ian agreed, "but he knew there was no future in farming. If the pair of you hadn't been so stubborn and proud, you might have found that out long ago without me having to pass on the message."

Jim opened his mouth to say something, but closed it again. He was deep in thought.

"Exactly what I've been saying all these years," Peg stood in the doorway, a steaming mug in her right hand. "The men in this family are too stubborn for their own good sometimes." She came in and sat down. "Seems like you two have been having quite the talk. About time if you ask me.

Here." She slid the mug of coffee over towards Jim. Ian's father took a sip. It looked as if he was about to say something when the Harbourmaster appeared in the doorway.

"Sorry to interrupt," he said, "but the girl who reported the lad drifting out the Pass has come over and I thought it would be nice for them to meet."

Ian looked up just as the Harbourmaster stepped aside. The light from the low sun almost blinded him. Squinting against it, he could see the silhouette of a girl in the doorway, her head surrounded by a halo of red hair.

"Hi," she said, stepping forward and holding out her hand, "nice to meet you. My name's Fiona."

The girl was Ian's age and tall. Her face was a mass of freckles — and very beautiful.

"Hi," Ian said as he shook her hand. "My name's Ian."

Fiona's smile broadened and she went on, "Mom and Dad and I are staying at the big white house on the beach. I saw you wave from the other side and then I saw you in the boat. I remembered my Dad saying how dangerous it could be out there, so I told Mr. Georgeson, he owns the white house, and he passed on the message. He works for the rescue service."

"And I am very glad he does," Ian said, "and thank you for acting so promptly. Who knows what would have happened or when they would have found me if I hadn't been spotted or if you hadn't reported it."

"No problem," Fiona said happily. Then she glanced

down. In embarrassed horror, Ian realized he was still holding her hand. He dropped it as if it were on fire. Fiona laughed. "Well, I'm glad you're okay," she said. "Maybe, when you've had a rest, you might want to drop over and meet Mr. Georgeson. You could tell us about your adventure."

"I'd like that," Ian said. "And thanks again."

Fiona's face broke into a smile that turned Ian's knees to jello. Then she turned and stepped out of the hut. Ian watched her go. Suddenly, he didn't feel in such a tearing hurry to leave the island.

# Epilogue

Ian stood gazing down at the collection of headstones in the corner of the small, well-kept cemetery. There were six of them. A lot of people weren't here; Billy and Becky were buried in Australia, Mary was probably in Nanaimo, Dorothy in Victoria, the first Donald over on the mainland somewhere, and Richard was only a name on some huge memorial in Belgium. But Ian was familiar with all those who were here; Ian and Mary in the same grave, Emily and Charlie side-by-side, little Sadie's sad plot, and his grandfather and mother. Would his parents be here one day? Would he?

It was a surprisingly warm morning considering it was the end of December. The four days here had all been like this, misty in the morning and with a few soft showers, but unseasonably warm. There had been plenty of opportunity for walks along the beach and even one afternoon calm enough for a short trip in the new aluminum rowboat, though Ian had been very careful about the tides.

Recently things had been going well. Physically, Ian had recovered very quickly from his night on and in Georgia Strait. Mentally and emotionally it was taking longer. He had gone through a stage of denying what had happened, putting the presence of ghosts down to an over-stressed mind and the effects of hypothermia. Despite what the helicopter observer had said, he had almost convinced himself that there was a rational explanation for it all when he saw the photograph. It was the old sepia one of Richard in his uniform, looking cocky and confident on his way to the horrors of the Great War. It sat, as it had always done, on top of the piano in the spare room. Ian had seen it thousands of times, but this time he remembered something Emily's ghost had said. Taking the photograph down, Ian eased it out of its old leather frame. He had to be careful because the paper was very brittle. Turning it over he saw the photographer's stamp, "James Adams, Photographer, Glasgow." Below that, in a flowing hand were written a few words that Ian knew by heart and which he could not have known from anywhere but Emily's ghostly lips, 'To Emily: doesn't your baby brother look grand in his new uniform?'

It had been a shock to see concrete proof that the ghosts had really visited him that night. Ian had spent long hours trying desperately to understand how it could have happened, but, eventually, he had given up and simply accepted that the impossible and unexplainable had actually occurred. It was much easier that way. Ian was even beginning to feel an urge to tell someone about his experiences.

He had begun to notice other things too, once he came to accept what had happened to him. The graves in front of him were one thing. He had never bothered to visit them before, but he knew the names and dates carved on the cold granite. The baptismal font in the little church was indeed a lump of natural sandstone from the beach and the minister had taken great delight in regaling Ian with the story of how the long-dead Cannon Paddon and three helpers had laboriously moved it up to the church. That had been the year before the Cannon's house had burned down and he, his wife, two daughters, and seven sons, had lost all their personal possessions.

Then there had been the haunting painting of gnarled windswept trees and driftwood on a beach somewhere on the West Coast of Vancouver Island. It hung in Ian's living room and was signed D. P. — Dorothy Park — the friend of Emily Carr and victim of the influenza epidemic of 1919. At the cabin there was a shelf by the back door where Ian could easily imagine Lee's money tin and in the corner of the yard was the old apple tree where the shadows even today suggested the crouching shape of a skinny old cougar stalking a child.

It couldn't be denied. It had all happened. Anything Ian could not have known before that night and could check afterwards turned out to be true. And Ian had checked, through all the island histories written by local historians.

He would never understand it, but he would always be grateful that it had happened. Learning about his family's past had made him a different person — more confident and, somehow, secure. He felt anchored in a way he never had before. School was working out fine and he was getting on much better with his father. Having a history in common, they had begun to talk. At first only about the family. Jim had told Ian all the stories he knew and Ian had absorbed all the information and fitted it into the pattern he already had. Occasionally, he would unthinkingly add something and his father would look at him strangely as if wondering how he could possibly have known that, but Ian had always managed to pass it off as a long-forgotten memory or something Jim had already mentioned.

Lately, the topics had broadened and each was discovering that the other was a human being with differences and similarities which made him worth getting to know. The tension had been washed away by the waters of Georgia Strait. Ian didn't feel adrift any more.

"There you are. Your folks have been looking for you everywhere. We have to get a move on if we're going to catch the ferry."

Ian turned to see Fiona coming towards him between the gravestones. He smiled.

"Yeah, I guess so. I was just saying good-bye to Emily. Let's go."

Linking arms the pair walked back to the cemetery gate.

"I should have known you'd be hanging around a bunch of dead people," Fiona continued. "I used to think it was weird the way you talked about your dead relatives as if they were still alive, but I guess some of them were pretty cool. Better than my boring old relatives anyway."

"Don't be so sure," Ian said with a smile, "you might be surprised what some of the boring old relatives can tell you."

"The ones that are still alive anyway," Fiona added.

Ian's smile broadened. He had gone over to visit Fiona at the white house on Gabriola and they had spent hours talking. Ian had never before met anyone who had seemed to understand him as well as Fiona did. Not that she was like him, she just understood him. He felt comfortable with her. He had also discovered that she lived quite close to him in Vancouver. They had hung out together quite a lot over the fall, and now Fiona had joined him for a four-day holiday at the old cabin on Mayne Island. It certainly didn't seem like a dull and boring place now. Ian laughed out loud.

"What's so funny?" Fiona asked.

"Oh, nothing," Ian replied. Then he added, "remind me one of these days and I'll tell you a ghost story."

Chattering happily the pair walked down the hill to the ferry terminal.

## AUTHOR'S NOTE

Many of the stories in *Adrift in Time* are true — there really was a Cannon Paddon on Mayne Island and Richard was killed by a shell on the slopes of Hill 70 in 1915. Liberties have been taken with time and place so that all the different tales can be fitted into one big story, but I hope no ghosts will come back to haunt me for changing things too much.

Most of these stories were taken from local history books of the Gulf Islands. There are many of them, often only available locally, and they are a rich source of narrative. Most particularly, I mined the history outlined in Peter Murray's delightful little book, *Homesteads and Snug Harbours: The Gulf Islands* (Horsdal & Schubart, Ganges, 1991).

# ABOUT THE AUTHOR

John Wilson, who was born in Scotland, is an ex-geologist and the author of more than a dozen successful fiction and non-fiction books for children and adults. He is also a freelance writer, book reviewer and published poet, and teaches occasional English courses at college and university level. In addition, John also conducts writing workshops and reads and tells stories from his books at schools and conferences. He lives on Vancouver Island with his wife and three children, and has never met a ghost.

**AGMV** Marquis

MEMBER OF SCABRINI MEDIA

Quebec, Canada
2003